FALLING IN LOVE

Catherine found herself relaxing as Philip talked to her of the lake, telling her how each season revealed its varied charms.

"I used to think I would never see anything more beautiful," he said. There was a smile in his eyes as he looked at her. She looked away, thinking with regret that she had never been paid so lovely or so subtle a compliment.

"Miss Arndale, I must thank you for all you are doing to teach Marianne and Lizzie."

"Your sisters are charming girls. It has been a pleasure teaching them," she replied, relieved at the change of subject. Now if only he would stop looking at her in such a dangerously affectionate manner . . .

"They are becoming very fond of you, and will miss you very much when it is time for you to end your stay here."

She looked down, troubled by the warmth in his voice. She knew he was referring to himself as well as his sisters. . . .

Books by Elena Greene

LORD LANGDON'S KISS

THE INCORRIGIBLE LADY CATHERINE

Published by Zebra Books

Dear Heather,
I hope you enjoy this
first of my "Three
Disgraces"!

THE
INCORRIGIBLE
LADY
CATHERINE

Elena Greene

[signature: Elena Greene]

ZEBRA BOOKS
Kensington Publishing Corp.
http://www.zebrabooks.com

ZEBRA BOOKS are published by

Kensington Publishing Corp.
850 Third Avenue
New York, NY 10022

All Kensington titles, imprints and distributed lines are
available at special quantity discounts for bulk purchases
for sales promotion, premiums, fund raising, educational or
institutional use.

Special book excerpts or customized printings can also be created to fit specific needs. For details, write or phone the office
of the Kensington Special Sales Manager: Kensington Publishing Corp., 850 Third Avenue, New York, NY 10022. Attn.
Special Sales Department. Phone: 1-800-221-2647.

Zebra and the Z logo Reg. U.S. Pat. & TM Off.

First Printing: September 2001
10 9 8 7 6 5 4 3 2 1

Printed in the United States of America

To my parents

One

A generous fire blazed in the drawing room of Maldon Park. In Cumberland, spring came later than in the gentler southern counties.

By the fire's strong but flickering light Philip Woodmere could see his friend Charlotte was embarrassed. Her mortification was easily accounted for; her family had thrust them together in the most disgustingly obvious manner. He glanced back at the group seated at the other end of the room. Though pretending to be absorbed in their cards, the Maldons were stealing curious glances their way, no doubt hoping for him to propose. They would probably be astonished if they knew that Charlotte had just rejected him.

Against his own expectations, she had refused his offer of marriage. A wave of intense, irrational relief surged through him, but he did his best to ignore it. He'd made an eminently sensible plan, in everyone's best interests. He had to persevere.

"Please tell me why you won't marry me," he said gently.

"Philip, we have always been good friends," she replied. "It is best that we remain so. What if you were to meet someone you truly loved? It could happen, you know."

He turned away from her, and looked into the fire for a few moments. Odd, how her words had stung a dormant fantasy of his back to vivid life for a moment. He had best forget it, though.

He reminded himself that it didn't matter that Charlotte was more likely to complain about the damp than admire the most sublime mountain view. It didn't matter that she would never thrill to the sound of a hawk keening over the fells, or understand why he sometimes stole out at night to enjoy the sight of Ullswater by moonlight, much less join him. Charlotte was kind and respectable, and sincerely cared for him and his family. He would find no more suitable bride.

"I'll probably never fall in love," he said. "But I'm sorry. For all I know you may still wish for a grand romance."

"Not at all," she replied with a suspicious degree of vehemence.

He didn't like the hopeless look in her gray eyes, or how it accorded with the sober color of half mourning she wore. Somehow, he had the conviction that her air of desolation was not entirely due to her father's death almost a year ago.

"Some coxcomb has hurt you," he said. "Why didn't you tell me, so I could have pitched him into the lake?"

"No one has hurt me," she replied, with a weak attempt at a smile. He cocked an eyebrow at her, and she relented. "He merely never thought of me."

He wondered briefly who it was that she had loved, and decided it would be rude to ask.

"Do you still cherish hopes of this man?" he asked.

"I do not."

"I am sorry," he said, hearing the sad finality in her

voice. He wondered if perhaps the object of her affections had already married.

They both stared into the fire for a few moments, then Philip broke the silence.

"I do not mean to press you, Charlotte, but perhaps you should consider marrying me. Your cousins do not value you as they should, and you know how much *I* need you."

He struggled to suppress the pain that still resurfaced at the thought of his parents' death. It had happened in the autumn, over a year ago, but as if it were yesterday, he could remember seeing them depart happily for a short visit with friends in Grasmere. It was on their return that a sudden storm had broken out, just as they were descending Kirkstone Pass, frightening the horses into a headlong bolt, causing the accident that left Philip and the rest of the family stunned with the suddenness of their loss.

All too vividly he remembered how his brothers and sisters had looked when he, the eldest, had struggled to break the news to them. He could still feel the bite of the cold wind that had blown the day his parents had been laid to rest in the Lynthwaite churchyard. He'd done his best to master his own grief, and to shoulder the responsibilities that had been thrust so abruptly on his then twenty-four-year-old shoulders.

There were times when his best did not seem good enough.

"I am sorry," said Charlotte softly. "I *do* understand."

"I've no worries about Jane or William," he said, reflecting on his two oldest siblings. "Jane is very happy with her husband in Derbyshire, and William seems to have been born for a life at sea. I can manage the younger boys, but the girls . . ."

"I know," said Charlotte with ready sympathy. "Marianne has grown very headstrong, hasn't she?"

"Another governess left us today." He sighed. "Marianne never used to be so troublesome. When I remember what she was like before the accident, I wonder . . . Perhaps it is only that she is sixteen."

"It is a difficult age. But surely your cousin can manage her?"

"Between us, I can say Cousin Dorothea is a very silly and quarrelsome woman. When Marianne misbehaves, Dorothea usually ends up blaming the governess, and Marianne doesn't mind either of them. I don't know what to do. If only my mother were alive! How should I know when a girl is ready to wear her hair up, and go to assemblies? And then there is Lizzie. She is only five years old. God knows I've tried to do my best by her—"

"And there you have succeeded thoroughly. I've never seen a more sunny-tempered child, and she adores you."

"Don't you see?" he asked impatiently. "She is so affectionate because she fears the people she loves will go away. She cries when I'm obliged to go away on business for a few days. She has terrible nightmares, too. I need someone—and not a mere servant—who can be with her always, to comfort her in the night. You could do that."

For a moment, it seemed to Philip that Charlotte was wavering. He supposed he should be pleased by it.

"Come, Charlotte," he continued. "You can't be comfortable in this household. Don't you think you would be happier at Woodmere Hall, surrounded by every comfort you could wish for, and family who care for you?"

"Thank you, but I have already made other plans," she replied. "Mama and I are going to remove to Maldon Cottage. I shall stay with her a few months, to help her become established there, but come summer I must advertise for a position."

"A position?"

"I am going to become a governess."

"A governess?" he asked, feeling a rising indignation.

"Yes. Mama's jointure is not sufficient to support us both."

"It was never meant to!" he protested. He softened his voice when he saw her wince. "I know as well as you that your papa always intended you both to continue living at Maldon Park with your cousins."

"He made no formal provision for that to happen, so Cousin George and Cousin Amelia can do as they wish."

"Even if it means turning you out of your home," he said grimly. "You had better marry me, then."

"No, Philip. I truly am sorry for your predicament, but I cannot marry you while my heart is given to another."

"Very well," he said. "I won't mention this again. In fact, I am sure we will both be more comfortable if we do not speak of this to your family. If over the next few months you should change your mind, let me know."

She looked grateful for his consideration, but said firmly, "I will not change my mind. Please do not hope for it."

Once again, he felt only relief at her refusal. He

chided himself for being selfish. What were his needs compared to his family's? Now that Charlotte had refused him, he'd have to look beyond the small circle of families in their valley to find a bride. Perhaps he could try to meet someone at the assemblies at Keswick or Penrith, but the prospect had little appeal. He might be considered a good catch by local standards, but he'd no desire to wed someone who only wanted the security he could provide her.

If he *did* meet a likely candidate, it would take time to get to know the lady and her family; time he didn't want to spend away from his family and lands. Then there was always the chance she would not wish to marry him. He was certainly no Adonis; no doubt he was too big and swarthy for a lady's taste.

He looked back at Charlotte. She was staring pensively into the fire again. He wished he could do more for her, but he had offered her all he could. Perhaps it was best he allow her to continue dreaming of her love, whoever he was.

Still, it was time he gave up such dreams himself. Once he had hoped to find a soul mate; now, he was reasonably sure she did not exist.

For the third time since she had entered the small salon, Lady Catherine Harcourt checked the time on the ornate clock on the mantelpiece. Her hostess, Lady Hetherton, had seen fit to light this little-used room in her London house with only a single branch of candles. By its light Catherine could see that it still lacked twenty minutes to midnight. She could faintly hear strains of music—a waltz—but the room seemed remote enough from the main activity of the ball for what she had planned. Tonight, if all went well, her life would change forever. For the better, she hoped.

If only her plan did not fail . . .

She resumed her restless pacing, but moments later she heard footsteps outside. Two ladies, one tall and golden-haired, the other a diminutive redhead, appeared on the threshold. Catherine smiled and ran to embrace them.

"So you received my messages! Did you have any trouble slipping away?" she asked.

"Not at all," said Juliana. "Pen tore a flounce, and I offered to help her pin it up. No one noticed we did not go to the ladies' retiring room."

"I never thought a propensity to destroy clothing would be so convenient," said Penelope with her fugitive, impish grin. "Well, I never wanted this dress anyway. It might look better if I were tall and beautiful, like you two. But I'm not, so it makes me look like an overdecorated pastry!"

Catherine looked at her sympathetically. There was no denying it; the myriad of ribbons and satin rosebuds decorating Penelope's gown did nothing to enhance her looks. Her short, slight figure was lost in the overtrimmed dress, and the pink rosebuds clashed vilely with her red hair. Moreover, Catherine saw that a rosebud was already missing from one of Penelope's flounces.

"Yes, I know there's a rosette missing," said Pen in a resigned tone. "We couldn't find it, and my aunt will undoubtedly scold me for being careless and ungrateful. But I never wanted this dress, or a Season for that matter!"

"You are not the only one whose relations have the most horrid taste," said Juliana. "Just look at me!

Grandpapa always has to see exactly what I am wearing before I ever leave the house, and make certain it is sufficiently ostentatious. With the result that I look like a jeweler's window!"

"It's not so bad," Catherine replied. "Sapphires and diamonds do suit you."

Juliana tossed her head, making the bejeweled butterflies in her hair sparkle. "Pooh! I feel like a walking advertisement: 'tradesman's heiress seeks peer of the realm for marriage, ranks above viscount preferred.' Besides, I wish I were dark like you. I look like a Dresden shepherdess—totally insipid!"

"I wish there was something I could do to help," said Catherine. "But you know *His Grace* will not even let me visit either of you. If he knew, I would be scolded just for talking to you now. Not that I care, of course."

Catherine watched the discontented faces of her school friends. This London Season, the first for her two friends, was just barely beginning, but already Juliana was restless and Penelope miserable. She hated seeing them so unhappy; they were the sisters of her heart, more like family than her own.

She had been desperately lonely her first months at Miss Stratton's select school. As the daughter of the Duke of Whitgrave, she had met with awe or thinly veiled jealousy from most of her schoolmates. Then Juliana had arrived, and Catherine had quickly discovered they shared the same sense of adventure. When Penelope came to the school a year later, shy and dowdy, still in mourning for the death of her parents, she had been instantly snubbed by the catty set. Catherine and Juliana had come to her rescue. Since then Pen, with her whimsical sense of humor, her imagination, and her generosity of spirit, had more than repaid their kindness, and everyone at the school developed a healthy respect for the "Three Disgraces," as they came to be known by the teachers and pupils alike.

Catherine knew that despite her rank, there was little she could do to help her friends at present. In her father and stepmother's eyes, the granddaughter of a Cit and an undistinguished orphan on the fringes of society were not fit companions for the daughter of a duke. The duke and duchess didn't—*couldn't*—understand that she would allow nothing to come between her and her old schoolmates. However, if all went well tonight, she would be free of such restrictions forever.

"So tell us what you are planning," said Juliana, breaking the unhappy silence. "Why did you ask us to meet you here?"

"I wanted to tell both of you before anyone else knew. I am eloping tonight. With Lord Verwood."

Both her friends stared at her for a moment. From their shocked expressions, Catherine deduced that they had heard at least some of the gossip surrounding the rakish baron.

Juliana was the first to recover. "What a delightful adventure! I wish you very happy."

Penelope looked thoughtful. "But, Cat—what about his reputation? Is it true what they say—that he once seduced and abandoned a young lady of quality?"

"He has assured me there is another side to the story, which he hopes to be able to tell me someday."

"Do you believe him?"

As she had done a number of times in the past week, Catherine thought back on the one private conversation she had had with Verwood, when he had taken her up in his phaeton for a drive about the park,

causing a minor scandal that had annoyed the duke
and duchess immensely. Verwood had behaved in a
perfectly gentlemanly manner, and had seemed hon-
estly sympathetic to her plight. His tolerant, easygoing
gallantry was a balm to her spirit after all that had
transpired last Season.

"Yes, I believe him," she replied. "I think Verwood
is not quite so black as he has been painted."

"Are you quite certain he is not a fortune hunter?"
asked Juliana.

"He has quite enough money of his own," Catherine replied. She decided it was not worth worrying her
friends with rumors that the Verwood fortune was out
of all proportion with the modest lands the family held
in Cornwall.

"Well, I suppose it *is* romantic," said Penelope.
"But are you sure you are in love with him, Catherine?"

Catherine paused before answering. Of her two
friends, Pen was the one who might detect the desperation beneath her bravado.

"In love?" she said, keeping her voice light. "No,
but I find him quite pleasant and amusing. We shall do
splendidly without love. He needs an heir, and cannot
bear the thought of marrying some silly miss who
would think to reform him. As for me, I shall gain my
freedom. Once we are married, no one will be able to
tell me I cannot read Byron, or play Beethoven. Or
whom I may or may not have as friends!"

Juliana looked envious, Penelope concerned.

"But what about love?" Penelope persisted. "You
always said you would marry only for love."

"That was before my first Season," said Catherine,

hoping Pen would not inquire further. "I know better now."

"We missed you so much last year," said Penelope shyly. "Miss Stratton's Seminary just wasn't the same without you. We always enjoyed your letters, and . . . well, we thought you were in love with Lord Staverton."

Penelope's soft words pried open the wound Catherine had been trying to ignore ever since last Season. She didn't wish to talk about it, particularly not tonight, when she needed all her courage.

"Love is not all it's cracked up to be," she replied after a pause. Then she saw the stricken look on Penelope's face, and regretted her cynical words.

"At least for me, it is not," she amended. "Things will be different for both of you, I'm sure."

"I can see you do not wish to tell us what happened last Season with Staverton," said Penelope in her gentle way. "But don't you think it is too soon to be running off with another gentleman?"

Catherine shook her head. She could not think about the possibility that she was making a mistake. She had made a plan, and there was no turning back. After yesterday's falling-out with her stepmother, the thought of another night under her father's roof was unbearable.

"I take it your father has refused his permission for you to marry Verwood," said Juliana.

"Of course. He is much too high a stickler to allow me to marry someone of such a reputation. Verwood tried to ask for my hand, but *His Grace* refused to even see him. My dear father has a far different sort of man picked out for me already. He wishes me to marry the Marquess of Hornsby."

"Lord Hornsby?" asked Penelope. "Who is he?"

"I am not surprised that you don't know. He almost never comes to London, for all he cares for is field sports. If I married him, I would be buried in the country all year-round, with no one but him and his horses and dogs for company."

"That doesn't sound so terrible," said Pen. "I thought you liked horses and dogs."

"I also like music, and poetry, and good conversation, but you will find none of those at Hornsby Hall. Besides, Hornsby is a fifty-year-old widower with no children. He regards me as he would a broodmare. On the one occasion that we met he told me he liked my bloodlines, and that I looked healthy enough to produce him any number of sons. He also said he had heard I was a headstrong filly, but he was sure he could break me to bridle soon enough!"

"How horrid!" said Penelope. "Of course you can't marry him, then."

"Are you leaving tonight?" asked Juliana.

Catherine nodded. "I am going to meet him in the conservatory at midnight," she said, glancing at the clock again. "If all goes well, we will be on our way to Scotland within the half-hour. I will write to you, the very first chance I get, for I am sure my family will do their best to hush things up."

"Well, I wish you luck," said Juliana. "Is there anything we can do to help?"

"Please just peek out into the hall before I go, and make sure my stepmother and stepsister are not about."

Her friends nodded. The Three Disgraces had run any number of rigs together during their time at school. Catherine could trust them to do much more difficult tasks than this.

She saw that Penelope was still looking troubled. Hiding her own rising agitation, she went over and hugged her tightly, kissing her on the cheek.

"Please do not look so worried, dear. I know what I am doing. Just wish me luck."

"Oh, I do. Believe me, I do."

The clock began to chime. Catherine released Penelope, then hugged Juliana in turn. Her friends quickly left the room, then motioned for her to come out. She did so, and took one last glance at the pair before making her way to the conservatory.

She tried to subdue the doubt that Penelope's words aroused in her. It was a desperate plan, but she was *not* afraid. She was taking charge of her own destiny. She hoped Juliana and Penelope would find the courage and means to do the same.

She paused on the threshold of the conservatory, and licked her lips, which had gone suddenly dry. She told herself again that she was not afraid. It was right that she and Verwood marry. He was a kindred spirit, another harsh, discordant note within the rigidly correct score of Polite Society. He would understand her as only a rake could.

Lifting her chin, and breathing a little fast in anticipation, Catherine entered the conservatory.

Two

Immediately, Catherine felt the warmth from the flues that provided the heat required for the exotic plants housed in the conservatory. Several torcheres illuminated the fanciful Gothic structure, highlighting the whites and pinks of the flowers, but leaving many shady nooks amongst the potted palms and other exotic shrubs. Somewhere at the opposite end was the doorway she and Verwood would use to start their flight.

Catherine took a deep breath, inhaling the earthy and sweet scents of the plants. It was the perfect place for an assignation; for a moment she could not help wishing she were meeting a man she truly loved.

But where was Verwood? Surely he would not fail her. He was the one who had arranged the details of their plan.

She heard a slight rustle behind one of the potted palms. She went eagerly toward the sound, then stopped cold as she heard an unexpected, but familiar voice.

"What a pleasure to meet you here, daughter."

Speechless with shock, she watched her father, the Duke of Whitgrave, step into the light. Now she could clearly see his receding silver-blond hair, and the blue eyes that were the single feature she had inherited from him.

"I suppose you will tell me you have developed a sudden passionate interest in botany," he said with heavy sarcasm.

She couldn't reply. The sense of shock gave way to a bitter combination of helpless rage and disappointment, and it threatened to overwhelm her. Her plan had failed, and she was sure to pay dearly for it.

She felt the beginnings of an inward trembling, and struggled to master herself so he would not see.

"What, have you nothing to say for yourself?" he asked, still in that same contemptuous voice.

Oh, why couldn't he just berate her like an ordinary angry father, concerned for her well-being! But he was not like other fathers, and it was foolish to waste time wishing things were different. She would not beg for his understanding, not again. She would not let him reduce her once more to the little girl who had once tried so hard to earn his affection.

"How did you know I would be here?" she asked, striving to keep her voice calm and level.

"You are impertinent as usual," he replied. "But I will tell you. I had the good fortune to intercept Verwood's note outlining this precious scheme. I sent him a response stating that you had reconsidered your decision to marry such a notorious rake."

Catherine felt her heart sink. Would Verwood believe the note? Would she ever have the opportunity to tell him she hadn't written it?

"I expect we shall not be troubled by Lord Verwood again," her father continued, with a look of satisfaction. "By the way, I have dismissed your maid. I keep no disloyal servants in my employ."

Poor Mariah! Catherine felt a stab of guilt for having involved her in this scheme. She had intended to bring Mariah with her to Verwood's household; now the poor girl would lose her position. It was useless to appeal to the duke to change his decision; Catherine would have to think of some other way to help Mariah.

First, she needed to understand what had happened.

"Why did you allow me to come here?" she asked, summoning up all her hard-earned self-control. "I am sure Mariah did not know you had intercepted the letter."

Only a slight tensing of his posture betrayed the duke's annoyance at her continued questioning.

"I wanted to see if you were brazen enough to go through with your plan. I should never have doubted it. You are hopelessly incorrigible. It is clear you are determined to blacken our family name."

Catherine thought of all the times her stepbrother Cedric and her stepsister Susannah had carried tales, true and otherwise, to her father and to her stepmother, and the inevitable punishments that had followed. Of the spiteful comments she had had to endure from the duchess and Susannah on the events of last Season. When she thought of what Her Grace had done just yesterday, Catherine could no longer contain herself.

"Why should I care about our precious name?" she asked. "When have I ever seen the smallest sign of affection from any of you? The happiest day of my life was when you sent me to Miss Stratton's!"

"Where you learned to make a vulgar exhibition of yourself at the pianoforte, and chose the most unsuitable of girls as your bosom bows!" he said. "You were such a difficult child, always running off by yourself. Your stepmother and I wanted to protect our children from being infected by your wild ways, and hoped the rigors of school would do you good. But I see now that we were mistaken."

Catherine bit her lip, determined not to show the pain his words caused her. She had learned two things at school: a degree of mastery over her temper, and some skill at the pianoforte. She had even been fool enough at one time to hope that he would be impressed with her accomplishments.

She should have known better.

"If you would just let me marry Verwood, I will trouble you no longer," she said, lifting her chin.

"I will not have you marry such a man. Nor can I allow you to remain in London and ruin your stepsister's first Season. No, since you made such a botch of matters with Staverton last Season, you must marry Hornsby. He is just the man to horsewhip you into shape."

"I will never marry Hornsby," she said. She straightened up, glad for once that she was tall, as her mother had been, so that she could look him eye to eye. She saw the raised veins in his forehead and the angry gleam in his eyes, and knew she had finally managed to break through his veneer of self-control.

"You disobedient hussy!" he spat, and slapped her. She recoiled from the sudden harshness of the blow, feeling tears prickle the back of her eyelids. She held them back. It was not the first time he had struck her. Doubtless he wanted her to grovel and cry. She would die first.

She saw him watch her, clearly frustrated by her lack of response. Then he reined in his fury with a visible effort.

"I am sure you will agree to marry Hornsby, once you know the alternative," he said coldly.

"What alternative? Are you sending me back to Whitgrave?"

"No, Verwood might try to pursue you there. I have a better plan. Your stepmother and I will tell everyone that your nerves have affected your health, and that you are in need of solitude and country air. Tomorrow, you will begin your journey to Cumberland, where you will visit with your great-aunts, the Arndale sisters. You may return when you agree to accept Hornsby's suit."

"I will never do so."

"We shall see. Do not imagine I am sending you on a pleasure expedition. I assure you Larkspur Cottage and the Vale of Lynthwaite are quite remote from the attractions of Windermere. There will be no visitors, no one but two eccentric old ladies to talk to. No horses to ride, no instrument to play. From what I recall of her, your great-aunt Matilda will be as strict a chaperone as I could wish.

"And I assure you, daughter, I am perfectly aware of all the times you and your cohorts escaped from Miss Stratton's Seminary. I have taken measures to ensure that you will be unable to repeat such a performance, and to prevent Verwood from seeking you out, should he try to do so."

Once again, her tears threatened to break forth, and again Catherine suppressed them. Her father had never been fond of her. Still, she had never imagined he would go to such lengths to be rid of her. Why?

"Why what?" he asked impatiently.

She realized then that she had spoken the word aloud.

"Why are you offering me such a choice?" she blurted. "How can you be so unnatural a father?"

He stared at her, no doubt appalled by the directness of her question. He also seemed at a temporary loss for an answer.

After a pause, he said stiffly, "I am convinced that your character is too unstable to withstand the excitements and temptations of Society. A quiet residence in the country will be in your best interests."

A rising indignation penetrated Catherine's wretchedness. How could he claim marriage with a man old enough to be her father would be to her benefit? His Grace was clearly lying; however, she could see by the expression on his face that he would tell her no more.

"So which will it be?" he continued. "Your greataunts or marriage to Lord Hornsby? It is your choice."

There was a triumphant note in his voice. A choking sense of despair possessed Catherine, as she realized he didn't care what she chose to do. He only wished her gone.

She was merely a nuisance, a problem to be solved. It was hopeless to think she could ever be anything more. As hopeless as wishing she had been a boy, or that her mother, the beauty she was said to resemble, had not died bringing her into the world.

"Come. It is time we returned home. Your stepmother has told everyone you have taken ill," said the duke, taking her by the arm.

On impulse, she tried to pull away.

"What do you think you are going to do?" he asked mockingly. "Run out into the streets of London penniless, and be taken for a doxy?"

Burning, she had to acknowledge the truth of what

he said. There was nothing she could do now. Silently, she followed him out of the conservatory.

She remained silent during the carriage ride back to Whitgrave House, knowing that tears or pleading would merely add to his victory over her. When they arrived at the ducal mansion, she listened impassively as her father gave orders to the footman to make sure she did not leave the house. The duke then returned to the carriage, and Catherine knew he was probably going to visit his mistress. The high standard of moral rectitude he expected from the ladies of his household did not extend to his own behavior.

Back in her own room, Catherine still could not give way to her feelings. First she had to try to console her distraught maid, and select several trinkets and articles of clothing that Mariah could sell to help tide her over before she found another position. It was a shame Catherine could not give her anything more valuable, but she knew Mariah would be accused of theft if she did so.

Finally alone, she paced the room, trying to think of a new plan. She was sure to be carefully guarded for some time. The duke would probably keep her whereabouts secret. She had no funds at her disposal, and no one to help her escape. She did not dare hope Verwood would make any effort to find her. It was even less likely that in the wilds of the north she would meet any man who would help her to the freedom she longed for.

She wished there were some way she could escape, and earn her own way under an assumed name. At her age, and without references, she would never be able to hire herself out as a governess. Besides, such a position was likely to be just as restrictive as life with her great-aunts. Her bent for music was of no use; no one hired a female to give concerts on the pianoforte, and her singing voice was nothing remarkable.

At a mental impasse, she stopped by the window, absently staring out into the gloom. As she thought again of the choice her father had offered her, she felt tears well up in her eyes. This time she allowed a few to fall before brushing them angrily away. She would think of something. Not tonight, but surely a new plan would come to her in time. Meanwhile, there was still something she had to do.

She pulled on a dressing gown and picked up her candle, then hurried down the stairs to the music room. She saw the cabinet where she had kept her music, and remembered how just yesterday her stepmother had sorted through it. Under the guise of concern for Catherine's reputation, the duchess had thrown all works that she deemed improper into the fire.

It didn't matter. Catherine's music mistress had called it a gift, her ability to commit to memory any piece of music after just one playing. Now Catherine thanked her stars for it.

She set her candle atop the beautiful instrument, and opened the lid. Lovingly, she ran a hand across its cool, smooth ivory keys, savoring the thought of the strings and hammers inside, ready to create whatever music she wished to call forth. She began to play, and for a time became unaware of anything else. She played sonatas, rondos, bagatelles, excerpts from concertos, anything and everything that was sweet, tragic, bold, or passionate.

At one point, between movements, she heard the voices of her stepmother and stepsister. They must have just returned from the ball. Now they were coming down the hall, no doubt with the intention of taunting her over her failed attempt to escape this curst household.

Immediately she launched into the finale to Beethoven's Sonata in C Sharp Minor, playing with demonic speed, sending the dark, surging arpeggios out into the house like a challenge. No one came, and she continued to play, asserting her defiance in rumbling bass notes and high staccato passages. She reached the end: descending arpeggios, rising back up to a trill and plunging down again. A weighty pause, and then the buildup to the grim conclusion.

When she finished, she realized the house was silent, and laughed aloud. The duchess and Lady Susannah already thought she was perfectly demented; no doubt they sensed her mood and were therefore afraid to come near her. Which was exactly what she had intended.

She continued to play, not knowing when she would again have the opportunity. All too soon, her candle sputtered out, leaving her in darkness. She closed the pianoforte and leaned forward, crossing her arms over the lid. Pillowing her head upon her arms, she awaited the dawn of her impending exile.

"Philip, have you heard the news?"

"No. Do tell me." Philip looked up from his dinner and smiled at Marianne. His sister's brown eyes were brimming with excitement, and her light brown curls bobbed as she spoke. She really was charming when she wasn't in one of her moods.

"There's a mysterious lady come to live at Larkspur

Cottage," she explained. "She arrived this afternoon, but no one knows who she is."

"It sounds like a fairy tale to me," he said, smiling.

"No, it isn't!" said Harry and Jack in unison. Harry stared Jack down, and continued. "It's the truth. A post chaise came from Troutbeck, and set her and four servants—or was it five?—down at Larkspur Cottage."

Jack chimed back in. "And Silas saw her over the garden wall. One of her servants is a huge giant of a fellow, and—"

"And she's the most beautiful lady Silas has ever seen," continued Marianne. "She's tall and as elegant as a goddess, with midnight black hair, alabaster skin, and deep blue eyes."

"I think she must be a princess in disguise!" cried Lizzie.

"See, I said it was a fairy tale," said Philip with mock severity.

As one, the children cried out in protest.

"Now, children, have you all forgotten your manners?" Cousin Dorothea tried to quell the din, but as usual, the children ignored her scolding.

"Quiet," he said after a few moments of pandemonium.

Instantly his siblings came to order.

"You may discuss the Arndales' mysterious visitor all you wish, but you must do so one at a time. 'Else there will be no picnic tomorrow morning."

He returned to his meal, listening in amusement as the children indulged in wild speculation about the nature of the mysterious lady at Larkspur Cottage. No doubt the shepherd who had seen her had exaggerated her beauty. No doubt there was a perfectly mundane explanation for her presence.

Still, it was odd. Philip had seen the Arndale sisters after church just a few days past, and they'd said nothing of a visitor, much less one who came with such a number of servants. In the small circle of local society, any newcomer created a stir; it was unlike the amiable old ladies to withhold such exciting news. He also knew that the sisters were daughters of a vicar, who had left them a small income barely sufficient for their needs. What relations did they have that could afford such an entourage?

The following morning brought additional news of the new lady at Larkspur Cottage, through the medium of the nursery maid returning from a day's holiday with her family in the village. The visitor was a Miss Arndale, great-niece of the Arndale sisters. She had come to the Lakes for her health, with a maid and a manservant, and was too great an invalid to mingle in local society.

His brothers and sisters discussed it all over breakfast, and quickly decided that the explanation was too dreary to be true. Lizzie thought the lady was a princess in hiding, while Marianne was of the opinion that she was the victim of a blighted love. The boys maintained that she must be a French spy until Philip pointed out that the war against the French had ended several years previously.

Though he smiled at these inventions, Philip also found it difficult to believe the tale of the Arndale sisters' invalid niece. He couldn't imagine that the limited society of Lynthwaite Vale could overexcite even a lady in delicate health. However, he kept his suspicions to himself.

After breakfast, they gathered up food and fishing gear, and set off for their favorite picnic spot, a meadow alongside a stream, now swollen by recent rains. The boys immediately began to fish; Marianne went into the nearby wood, ostensibly to look for wild-flower bulbs.

Seeing the older children happily occupied, Philip lifted Lizzie onto his shoulders and took her for a brisk ride. He was glad he'd organized this outing, the first of the season. He wouldn't forego these pleasures for anything: the mild sunshine, the crisp morning air, Lizzie's little arms around his neck, her delighted shrieks as he jumped imaginary obstacles in their ca-reer about the meadow.

Soon enough, however, his enjoyment was inter-rupted by the all-too-familiar sounds of conflict rising above the sound of the rushing stream. Quickly, he set Lizzie down near Marianne and asked the older girl to mind her. Marianne protested the charge, but he ig-nored her, running toward the source of the commo-tion.

He came around a bend, where he saw the boys wrestling in the mud near the stream's edge.

"Stop it this instant," he commanded, and pulled Harry off Jack.

"But he cast his line right over mine!" complained Harry.

"I did not!" said Jack. "I wouldn't have done it if you weren't trying to take all the best spots in the stream for yourself!"

"I don't care whose fault it is. If you two can't keep from fighting, I'll take both your rods away."

As he knew they would, the two subsided into frus-trated muttering and slunk to separate spots along the stream bank.

He came back around the bend into the meadow.

Glancing around, he saw that Marianne had sat down
in the crotch of a willow tree beside the stream and
had opened up a book. No doubt one of the lurid nov-
els she favored. He wondered if he should allow her to
read so many of them. On the other hand, the restric-
tion would probably goad her into worse rebellion.

But where was Lizzie?

He looked further downstream. To his horror, he
saw his youngest sister a few hundred yards away,
holding a toy boat in her hand while walking precari-
ously along a log that had fallen over the stream. He
choked back the angry warning that arose in his
throat, not wanting to startle her.

But it didn't matter. Lizzie tottered, dropped the
boat, and waved her arms wildly. With a frightened
cry, she fell into the rushing stream.

Three

The sound of birds chirping outside her window penetrated Catherine's consciousness like a sweet, almost forgotten memory of childhood. Still half asleep, she stretched, enjoying the birdsong and the dappled morning sunlight.

Then she remembered where she was.

Surreptitiously, she rolled over and observed the woman lying on the trestle bed in front of the door. Jemima Grimsby was still sound asleep, and even from across the room Catherine could smell the gin on her breath.

She was not surprised; during the journey from London she had learned the truth about the servants her father had appointed to accompany her to Cumberland, that Grimsby hailed from an asylum for the insane, while her male cohort, Ned Leach, had been a keeper at Newgate gaol.

A gnawing anxiety arose in the pit of Catherine's stomach as she pondered the extreme measures the duke had taken to prevent her from running away. She suppressed the feeling, reminding herself that he knew all about her escapades at Miss Stratton's school. No doubt, he thought this was what was necessary to keep her in check. It had to be just that simple; there could be no more sinister motive behind these harsh measures.

Still, when the duke had hired Grimsby and Leach, he must not have been aware of their penchant for strong drink! Over the past week, during their journey from London, Catherine had noticed her guards gradually relax their caution. She had fostered their carelessness. By sleeping late every morning and complaining about the food and beds at all the inns along the way, she had managed to convince them she was a fragile, pampered, helpless lady of fashion.

During the journey north Grimsby and Leach had limited their drinking, but last night, they had decided they could celebrate the occasion of her safe delivery to Larkspur Cottage. Now it was time to take advantage of their laxness.

She slipped silently out of bed and tiptoed to the wardrobe. She pulled out a simple gown and a warm cloak. Quickly, she dressed herself, then pulled on a pair of sturdy half boots. There was no knowing how far she would have to walk.

The bed creaked as she sat down to lace up her boots, and she winced at the sound. She glanced back over at Grimsby, but the woman continued to snore heavily. Catherine wondered if a regimental band playing their loudest would be sufficient to awaken the woman, and swallowed a nervous chuckle.

Now it was time for the trickiest part of her escape. Grimsby had taken Catherine's small jewelry box to bed with her, but Catherine was fairly certain she would be able to pry it loose, given the woman's present state of intoxicated lethargy.

Unfortunately, there was nothing of great value in the box. Catherine's father had expected her to be expensively adorned in London, as befit the daughter of a duke, but before she had left her stepmother and stepsister had taken the most precious pieces. Between their depredations and the items she had given to Mariah, there were only a few trinkets left. Hopefully, they would fetch a decent enough price to pay her way back to London.

Holding her breath, Catherine slipped the box out from Grimsby's loose hold. Her heart stood still as Grimsby stirred and muttered, only to resume its normal pace as the woman rolled over and snored with renewed vigor.

She tiptoed back toward the window and opened it, startling the birds that had been perched in the tree growing just outside her room. She smiled as she saw a sturdy branch growing at an angle along the cottage, just above the level of the window, then suppressed another laugh. Grimsby and Leach had clearly not anticipated that the fashionable young lady in their charge would do anything so bold as climbing out of a window and using a tree to make her escape. Compared to the time the Three Disgraces had run away from school to attend a fair, this was too ridiculously easy!

Still, she would need both hands. Carefully, she dropped the jewelry box out of the window. It fell silently onto the soft lawn in the small garden behind the cottage. She leaned out the window, grasped the welcoming branch, and swung herself out. She inched her way toward the trunk, cursing softly as her skirt caught on a smaller branch. The last time she had climbed a tree it had been in borrowed boys' clothing. This was harder.

A few moments later, she reached the trunk and

stopped to listen. She could still hear Grimsby's snoring. She dropped her feet to rest on the next lower branch, then sat down upon it, and dropped the remaining distance onto the springy grass.

She picked up the jewelry box and hurried to the gate in the stone wall. She could hear sounds from the kitchen; her aunts' maid Jenny preparing breakfast, and the blustering voice of Ned Leach. She had best make her escape quickly.

Still, she turned back for one more look at the cottage, feeling unexpected regret at leaving her great-aunts without a good-bye. Despite having her foisted upon them without notice, they had been touchingly kind in their own ways.

On the other hand, both the Arndale sisters were clearly uneasy about Catherine's villainous entourage, and displeased with the letter her father had sent, detailing the restrictions he wished to be placed around her. No doubt Aunt Matilda and Aunt Phoebe, like everyone else, would feel mostly relief to see her gone.

She passed through the gate to the lane and turned left, making her way down the lane that meandered down toward the main road out of the valley. As she walked, she reviewed her plan of action.

Leach and Grimsby were sure to search for her; it was imperative that she concoct some sort of disguise to throw them off her path. Ruefully, she had decided that masquerading as a boy was no longer a possibility as it had been in her earlier years at Miss Stratton's school. Her best course would be to go to the next village, purchase some simple clothing, and travel on the stage, posing as a country girl going to London to seek a position. Yesterday, she had listened carefully to

Jenny's speech; she was sure she could mimic the accent. A little acting combined with the proper attire should do the trick.

When she reached London, she would contact Verwood. If he believed the note the duke had sent him, he might already be looking about for another lady to suit his purposes. Impossible that she could do the same in this godforsaken district. Even if she were allowed to meet any of the men who lived here, she was sure she would find them uncouth sportsmen, no better than Lord Hornsby.

No, Verwood still presented her best chance for freedom.

Her spirits rising, Catherine increased her pace. For the first time, she looked about her. She had arrived yesterday evening under the gloomy cover of a spring rainfall, so she had gained only the haziest impression of the landscape.

The lane ran in easy curves down toward the main road through the valley. All around her, high hills rose, some wooded, most covered only with bracken or sheep. Somewhere close by lay Ullswater; the lake might even be visible from some of the nearby hilltops. There was a clean, fresh smell in the air; she almost wished she had time to explore. She had always wanted to see the Lakes, although not like this. Perhaps she could come back here someday.

"Ho, there, me lidy! Not so fast! Don't think you can run away from Ned Leach so easy!"

Catherine started at the unwelcome sound of Leach's voice, shouting in the distance. Blast! Grimsby must have awoken after all, or perhaps Leach had seen her from the kitchen window.

She turned, and saw he was still some distance

away, Grimsby running still further behind. Even at a distance she could hear them swearing and panting. Evidently, their previous lives had not prepared them for running along rough country lanes, and presumably last night's overindulgence in gin did not improve their speed. She still had a chance!

She ran as quickly as she could, and soon reached the main road. Last night she had tried to memorize the last few turnings of the coach. Hoping she had remembered correctly, she turned right, and made her best speed down the muddy road. A quick glance behind showed her that Leach and Grimsby were still in pursuit, and they had seen which way she'd turned.

She looked about, and saw a stile through the hedge on the left side of the road. Quickly, she scrambled over it. She skidded a little in the muddy patch on the other side, then began to run across the pasture toward a line of trees on the other side, scattering sheep as she went.

Partway across the pasture, she looked back and suppressed a nervous laugh. Leach had stumbled descending from the stile, and fallen in the mud on the near side. Clearly, the night's overindulgence hadn't increased his agility.

She continued running and reached the relative cover of the trees, which were still more thinly clad at this season than she would have liked. She turned to see that Leach was now struggling to extricate his boot from the mire. Grimsby was not in sight.

Looking around, Catherine realized she had several choices. The woods bordered a swift stream. There was a path running alongside the stream in both directions. A wooden footbridge crossed the stream. Three possible routes. Which one to take?

She had no idea of the geography of the valley. She only knew that if she went to the right, she would be able to retrace the route that the carriage had taken to bring her here. However, that was no good; surely one of her pursuers would go that way. She would have to go left, and pray that the path led to some village or other.

Quickly, she ran forward through the soft ground near the footbridge, making the deepest prints she could so that it would appear that she had taken that route. Before she reached the footbridge, she leapt to her left and ran lightly over the overgrown edge of the path along the side of the stream, praying she had made the right choice.

She ran on for perhaps a half-mile, looking back occasionally to make sure there was no one following. Finally, her legs began to tremble from the effort, and she slowed to a walk. It seemed she had thrown Leach and Grimsby off her path, at least temporarily. She felt a rumbling in her stomach, and wondered how far she would have to go to reach the next village.

Nevertheless, freedom felt wonderful. There was a delightful breeze, just enough to move the gossamer beginnings of leaves on the trees skirting the path. Beneath them, Catherine saw the pale golden blossoms of primroses and the occasional drift of wood anemones, like little white stars scattered beneath the tree roots.

Then the silence of the woods was broken by the sound of a high-pitched scream, followed by a splash. Catherine turned toward the rushing stream, and saw a small, dark head bobbing just above the water about a hundred yards away.

Good God! It was a little girl, her arms thrashing wildly, caught in the current. Coming her way, Catherine realized. If she moved quickly she would be able to rescue her.

She dropped her jewelry box and half ran, half fell down the steep slope to the water's edge. She plunged in, gasping as the frigid water surrounded her. Willing herself to ignore the cold, she waded on, aiming for the spot where she thought the current would carry the child. The stream was deeper than she had expected, coming up almost to her chest.

Abruptly the current swept the child into Catherine's arms, almost knocking her over. Catherine held the little girl tightly, but in her panic the child continued to thrash about, spluttering and coughing all the while. For a few frenzied moments, Catherine felt the water catch at her heavy woolen cloak, dragging them both along for a few yards.

Somehow, she managed to undo the clasp and release the cloak. Freed of its dragging weight, she worked to regain her balance. Miraculously, her feet came up against a large stone in the streambed. She was able to brace herself against it, but that was all she could do while the little girl continued to flail her arms.

"I have you . . . safe now," she said, gasping for breath. "But . . . you must stop struggling. Do you understand?"

The little girl quieted and looked up at her, large brown eyes wide with fear. She nodded.

"Good girl," said Catherine. Feeling for each foothold, she started to make her way to the bank. She found the return much harder. Not only had the current swept them into a deeper section of the stream, but she had the burden of the shivering child to carry. Her legs, already taxed by her run, began to feel heavy and numb with the cold.

Then she heard several voices shouting from the stream's edge. Standing out among them was a deep, masculine voice.

"Stay there! I'll come and get you. Harry, fetch the blanket!"

Relief flooded through Catherine. Gratefully, she stopped, and concentrated on the easier task of maintaining her position against the current.

"H—hurry, p—please!" cried the little girl, her teeth chattering.

"I'm coming, Lizzie. Don't worry!" the man shouted.

Catherine turned her head and saw a brawny, dark-haired man wearing a white shirt and buckskins plunge into the stream and stride toward them, the current parting in waves around his broad chest. In another instant he reached them.

He took the child and held her close to his side, putting his other arm around Catherine. She felt a new strength course through her, as if he had lent her some of his own.

"Just a little further, miss," he said in an encouraging tone, and the three of them set off toward the bank. There Catherine saw a boy and an older girl awaiting them. As they reached the shallows near the edge of the stream, a second boy ran up, carrying a blanket.

Catherine breathed a deep sigh of relief. They had come to safety. Still, as she looked up the steeply sloping bank, she realized that getting back up it would be more difficult than coming down had been.

The man released her then.

"I'll be back for you," he assured her, and climbed up the bank. He handed the little girl over to the others, who immediately wrapped her up, then turned to help Catherine. As he looked down at her, he froze.

She stared back. He was tall, burly, and broad-chested. In fact, every part of him was broad, even his face. Wide-nosed, swarthy, coarse. He looked positively barbaric. Except for his eyes, perhaps, which were large, and a warm dark brown, like those of the little girl she had just helped rescue. As she stared, their expression changed from concern to naked admiration.

Then she realized how her flimsy, wet gown was clinging to her body. She blushed, feeling suddenly warm despite the cold water dripping off her. How dare he stare at her so? Who was he anyway? The village blacksmith, by the look of him.

"Well?" she asked. "Are you going to help me or must I scramble up by myself?"

"I'm sorry, miss," he said, his face reddening. The trace of a northern brogue in his rich baritone voice gave further confirmation to her assessment of his rank. She had never heard a gentleman speak so.

He reached a hand down, and helped her up the steep slope. She slipped at the top, and he put his arms around her to steady her. Although he had been in the same stream, he didn't feel cold at all. Catherine felt an all-too-familiar, dangerous warmth steal through her. She could not let it distract her from her purpose. Abruptly she pulled away.

"Unhand me!" she demanded, but by the time she got the words out he had already released her. Immediately she began to shiver.

Annoyed, she saw him turn to examine the little girl he'd called Lizzie. Beyond him, she saw the older girl sitting on the ground, sobbing, and the two boys standing by, worried frowns on their young faces.

"Lizzie will be perfectly well," the man assured them. "We just have to get her home and into dry clothes.

He turned back toward Catherine, and picked up a coat from the ground. He wrapped it around her, and she relaxed slightly, relieved to be more decently covered, and much warmer, for the coat went around her almost twice.

"Is that better?" he asked gently.

She nodded, revising her assumptions. Though not in the height of fashion, his coat was of excellent quality. Perhaps he was a well-to-do farmer.

"Philip Woodmere, at your service," he said. Although his bow lacked polish, she saw that he moved with an innate strength and grace. Which was of not the slightest consequence, she reminded herself, as she tried to think of a reply. He clearly wanted to know who she was, but could she tell him?

Now that she was wet through, she needed his assistance. Would he be willing to provide her with some dry clothes and let her go on her way without asking any questions? Could she afford the delay?

While Catherine hesitated, Mr. Woodmere glanced over at the little girl, and then looked back at Catherine.

"My family and I thank you," he said. Beyond him she saw the others staring at her, eyes wide with mingled curiosity and something that looked like budding hero worship.

"I hate to think what would have happened if you had not been by," Mr. Woodmere continued. His voice broke, and despite her own quandary, Catherine was touched.

"Well, Mr. Woodmere, perhaps you should not allow your daughter to play unattended by a stream," she answered sharply, to cover her emotion.

"I didn't think my *sister* was unattended," he replied, frowning. "Now we must get you and Lizzie back to Woodmere Hall and into dry clothing as quickly as possible, Miss . . . ?"

Oh, why hadn't she thought of a false name to use? She quickly looked about her for inspiration. After a short pause, she replied.

"Brook."

He frowned again; she could see he was suspicious. However, he only said, "Very well, Miss Brook. Shall we go?"

"Not so fast!" shouted a gruff voice behind them. Catherine turned around, and felt a desperate fury choke her as she saw Leach and Grimsby jogging down the path in their direction, looking tired but with dogged looks on both their faces.

"And 'er name is Miss Arndale."

"It is not! I am—"

"An' it's 'igh time she got back 'ome to 'er aunts," shouted Grimsby, drowning out the end of her sentence.

Catherine fell silent. Mr. Woodmere looked perplexed. Obviously he was trying to decide whom to believe. Oh, why had she lied to him and behaved in such a haughty manner?

"To Larkspur Cottage?" he asked, looking at Grimsby and Leach. "Woodmere Hall is closer. As you can see, she is wet through. My sister can lend her some dry clothing, and I can send her home in our carriage."

"Thank ye, sir, but she's to go wi' us," said Leach, watching Mr. Woodmere anxiously. He and Grimsby came up on either side of her.

"Miss, er, Arndale? Would you rather come home with us?" asked Mr. Woodmere. He seemed torn, looking at her and then at his little sister, who was visibly shivering under the blanket.

Catherine shook her head. It didn't matter now. Clearly, he had guessed that she had lied about her name. After that, he probably would not believe her if she told him it wasn't Arndale, either. Besides, even if she went to his home, Leach and Grimsby were sure to come along and make sure she returned. No doubt they would also increase their vigilance after this. Once again she had not only failed to make her escape, she had made matters worse.

She slumped, suddenly overwhelmed by despair and physical exhaustion. She looked back up to hear Mr. Woodmere bid her farewell.

"Good-bye, Miss Arndale, and thank you again," he said. "If there is ever anything I can do for you, just send word to Woodmere Hall and be sure that I will come to your aid."

He picked up Lizzie, then he and the rest of his family walked off. Catherine turned her head to watch them go, even as Leach and Grimsby marched her off in the opposite direction.

She felt her depression lift slightly. There had been a warmth in Mr. Woodmere's voice, and in the depths of his brown eyes. He hadn't been put off by her haughty behavior or her lie, after all. Perhaps he *could* help her somehow.

Philip could not resist a backward glance at Miss Arndale, even as he hurried homeward with his family. There had been something starkly tragic about her expression when her servants had arrived to escort her home. In the distance, he saw her walking defiantly upright between the strange pair, oddly like a prisoner being escorted to gaol.

"See! She *is* just like a princess, isn't she?" said Lizzie, snuggling in his arms.

"Yes, she is."

"Philip? I'm sorry I fell in the water."

"I forgive you," he said, smiling down at her. Thank goodness she seemed not to have taken a chill. He did not miss his own coat at all; he was still warm from his encounter with Miss Arndale.

"Thank goodness Miss Arndale was there," said Marianne, tears continuing to spill down her cheeks. "I'm so s—sorry, Philip. I know I should have been watching Lizzie. I shall never be so careless again!"

"I hope not," he said sternly, then reminded himself that he and Cousin Dorothea were also at fault. Seeing his sister's distress, he relented. "There's no need to cry, Marianne. Lizzie is safe."

Marianne still looked dejected, and the boys seemed subdued.

"You three can run ahead," he told them. "Tell Cousin Dorothea what has happened, and make sure she orders a good fire in the nursery before we get there."

Marianne and the boys ran ahead, all looking relieved to have tasks to do. Lizzie lay quietly in his arms, exhausted from her adventure. Philip was left with his thoughts, which were more disordered than they had been in years.

It wasn't Lizzie's brush with disaster that was playing havoc with his emotions, either. He'd become as accustomed as anyone could be to his brothers and sisters' harebrained exploits. No, it was Miss Arndale that occupied his mind.

When he had first caught sight of her holding Lizzie in the stream, he'd felt intense relief to see Lizzie being aided, and a desperate fear that they might both be swept away. Then he'd seen Miss Arndale's face as she struggled to bring Lizzie safely to shore. Her strong, pure features held an expression of fierce determination, and he had known beyond a doubt that she would have succeeded in bringing Lizzie to shore alone.

He'd waded in to help her, and as soon as he'd put his arm around her, an intense sensation, almost like a blow, yet pleasurable, pervaded his being. It had been a wrench to let her go at the bank so he could get Lizzie up. Then she had looked up at him with stormy blue eyes, and he'd completely lost his senses for a moment, forgetting his family, the stream, everything but this wild, lovely creature in her dripping, clinging gown.

She'd spoken sharply, recalling his wits, but as he steadied her on the slope, the earlier feeling had returned, even more strongly, until she was obliged to scold him again. And rightly so, he thought ruefully. He should not have stared at her like a callow schoolboy, rather than the mature, respectable gentleman he knew himself to be. He'd managed to drag his eyes away from her enticing form, but his heart had continued to pound as he'd tried to thank her for what she had done. Again she'd thrown cold water on his friendly overtures, even lying about her name.

She was an enigma, this visitor to their remote valley. Why was she here? The earlier story was clearly wrong; no lady in delicate health could possibly have done what she had. There was something strange about those servants of hers, too. The man in particular seemed more like a hired ruffian than a servant. Were the three of them in league to take advantage of the Arndale sisters somehow?

Philip rejected the lurid suspicion. It didn't make any sense; the Miss Arndales were not wealthy. And from the way the younger Miss Arndale (if that was indeed her name) had looked at him as the others took her away, it was clear she was not a coconspirator. Her expression had been defiant and yet desperate somehow, like a silent plea. For what?

What was her secret? What did she want?

He longed to know, and yet into his eagerness crept a sense of foreboding at what he might discover. If it were only himself at risk, he would throw caution to the winds. But he was not free to pursue any quixotic quest he wished. He had brothers and sisters to establish; he could not embroil them in any trouble that might reflect badly on them, or affect their chances.

Lizzie stirred in his arms as they approached home. Philip hugged her closer. The pang of having almost lost her reminded him of the magnitude of the debt he owed Miss Arndale. He *had* to find a way to repay her. Surely he was levelheaded enough to do so without compromising his family's well-being.

Still, his blood rushed at the thought of seeing her again.

Four

Grimsby and Leach grumbled at Catherine all the way back to Larkspur Cottage. She ignored them, knowing that their heads must be aching from last night's debauch, and that any reply would only anger them more. She preferred to be left to her own thoughts at any rate.

Her mood, temporarily lifted by Mr. Woodmere's parting words, plummeted again as she considered her situation. Of course she could not regret having stopped to help his little sister. Thank God she had been able to do this one good deed. However, now that Grimsby and Leach knew she was no frail flower it would be difficult, not to say impossible, to escape again without help. But what would Mr. Woodmere do for her, after all?

He was Woodmere of Woodmere Hall. It sounded so very settled, so dreadfully respectable. A gentleman farmer, responsible for a horde of brothers and sisters. This was surely not a man who would lend himself to any scandalous undertaking.

No, she could expect nothing from him, despite the fact that she felt a wanton pleasure in the memory of his arms, in the warmth and lingering masculine scent of his coat. No doubt he would be shocked and appalled if he knew that her sharp words had only been

an attempt to hide her unwanted, treacherous reactions
to his manly appeal. Perhaps it was just as well she
was unlikely to see him again.

They rounded the final bend in the lane, and Larkspur Cottage came into view. Catherine gazed once
more on its slate roof bedecked with mosses and li-
chens, its walls covered in places by the budding vines
of honeysuckle and creeping roses, its tiny lawn sprin-
kled with daffodils and crocuses. A charming picture.

A very pretty cage.

As they turned up the path toward the cottage, the
front door, painted a cheerful bright green, flew open.
Catherine's great-aunts came out to meet them.

Aunt Phoebe was the first to reach Catherine, her
impetuous quickness and her delicately sprigged gown
of pale lilac seeming to belie her silvered hair and
wrinkled face.

"Thank heavens you are safe! We were *so* fright-
ened for you," she cried, putting her arms around
Catherine. "Oh dear, you are soaked to the skin!
Whatever happened?"

"I am sorry. It—it is a long story," she replied,
guilt-stricken at Aunt Phoebe's warm reception. She
had never thought they would worry so.

"Come in quickly, then, before you both catch your
death!" scolded Aunt Matilda, close behind Aunt
Phoebe. She was the elder of the two, taller and even
thinner than her sister, and looking rather like a disap-
proving crow in her dark gown. "You will tell us what
happened once you are dry and warm again."

Aunt Matilda then addressed herself to Grimsby
and Leach, "You two good-for-nothings! Make yourselves useful. You—build up the fire in the sitting
room, and, you—tell Jenny to make some tea and

bring it there. Well, why are you standing about and gaping? Surely you do not wish to explain to His Grace why his daughter succumbed to an inflammation of the lungs while in your care?"

Catherine watched in amazement as Leach, that hulking ogre of a man, hurried off into the sitting room. Grimsby disappeared with equal speed in the direction of the kitchen. Meanwhile her aunts towed Catherine upstairs. Bemused, she allowed them to help her change into dry clothing, Aunt Phoebe cooing over her, and Aunt Matilda scolding, both with equal concern.

She had not been fussed over so since childhood, before her favorite nursemaid had been turned off for taking Catherine's part in some squabble with Susannah. It was both touching and mortifying. She didn't deserve such kindness, after having run away so rudely.

A short while later, she sat in a wing chair in the cozy sitting room and devoured some delicious oaten cakes with her tea. When Catherine finished her belated breakfast, Aunt Matilda began the expected inquisition.

"Now, Catherine," she said, with a grim expression, "you must tell us how it comes about that you left us, and why you have returned to us soaked to the skin."

Catherine had trouble meeting Aunt Matilda's sharp eyes. "There was a child who had fallen into a stream. I helped to rescue her," she replied.

"So brave of you, dear Catherine!" said Aunt Phoebe. "It is a wonder you did not both drown!"

"Well, it was not so very deep, but oh it was cold! I think I could have gotten us out well enough on my own, but I admit I was pleased when her brother, Mr. Woodmere, came and helped us out."

"Oh, was it little Lizzie who fell in? How is the darling child?" asked Aunt Phoebe.

"I think more frightened than anything else," said Catherine. "They wrapped her up very quickly. I think she will not take a chill."

"Well, I am very glad you were there to help her, but I cannot conceive what you were doing by the stream."

"Don't be a goose, Phoebe! Catherine did not climb out of her window for a stroll. She was running away from us, of course," said Aunt Matilda.

"Oh no! Can it be true, Catherine?" asked Aunt Phoebe, a hurt look in her eyes, pressing one hand to her heart. "We had hoped you would be so happy with us! Why, year after year we asked your father to allow you to spend a summer here, and we were so over-joyed when you finally arrived on our doorstep. The very image of your dear mother!"

Aunt Phoebe looked to be on the verge of tears. Catherine felt like the cruelest wretch. She had never meant to harm anyone, and now her great-aunts were suffering for her escapades, just as poor Mariah had.

Agonized, she sprang up from her seat and knelt down before Aunt Phoebe, gathering a withered old hand into her own. "I'm sorry, Aunt Phoebe. I never meant to worry you so!"

"You behaved in a very thoughtless, selfish manner, Catherine," said Aunt Matilda. Catherine looked up to see her elder aunt eyeing her sternly. "It is lucky this incident has not brought on one of your Aunt Phoebe's *palpitations!*"

Appalled, Catherine looked back at Aunt Phoebe.

Her great-aunt had a weak heart? Small and thin-boned, Aunt Phoebe looked so fragile that a sharp wind could have blown her away. Oh, why hadn't she noticed?

"I—" Aunt Phoebe began. She looked at Aunt Matilda, and then back at Catherine, her cheeks turning pink. "I do not like to have it spoken of. I do not wish to appear an invalid. Please do not berate Catherine, Mattie. She did not know, and I am sure she meant no harm."

"She needs to understand the consequences of her actions," said Aunt Matilda.

"I do, Aunt Matilda. I am so sorry. You have both been more than kind to me, and indeed I am grateful, but I must—I have reasons why—I wish to return to London."

"Your father wrote us about Lord Verwood," said Aunt Matilda. "He sounds like a veritable ne'er-do-well and you had best put him out of your mind."

"Oh no, dear Mattie, how can you be so unfeeling? Catherine is in love. Indeed, how can we be so certain that the duke is in the right about the young man?" said Aunt Phoebe, patting Catherine's head in a manner that was exasperating and touching at the same time.

She dared not draw away. How could she tell them she was *not* in love with Verwood? Poor Aunt Phoebe would be so hurt if she knew Catherine's escape did not have such a romantic motive.

"Men are swine," said Aunt Matilda categorically. "I am sure Verwood is no exception. The duke has given us strict instructions to keep him and other undesirable gentlemen away from Catherine, and I shall make certain his orders are followed."

"You cannot wish to keep Catherine from her true love. She might fall into a decline!"

Aunt Matilda snorted. "She won't fall into a decline over a foolish infatuation. She's more like to come to grief trying to run away to him again."

"I cannot bear to think of it," said Aunt Phoebe. "Dear Catherine, you might have broken your neck climbing out of that window, or drowned in the stream! You must promise not to try to run away from us again."

Catherine felt herself being ensnared once more. Somehow the fact that it was all in kindness made it almost harder to endure. She got up, and began to pace about the modest room, already feeling unbearably confined within its four narrow walls.

"You do not wish to be the death of your Aunt Phoebe, do you?" asked Aunt Matilda, halting Catherine in her tracks.

She turned back toward her aunts. Aunt Phoebe stared up at her with a pathetically eager expression. Catherine was shocked to see that even Aunt Matilda's eyes were suspiciously bright. She took a deep breath, struggling to suppress the futile, rebellious feelings that rose up in her heart.

"No, of course not," she said. "I promise you I will not try to run away again."

Aunt Matilda made a careful scrutiny of Catherine's face, then nodded. "I am glad you have decided to be sensible. I believe we may trust you. You have a great look of your mother, and whatever else, she was always truthful."

Catherine sat back down, feeling drained by the emotions of the day. Now it seemed she would have to accustom herself to a period of seclusion with her great-aunts. She owed them at least a short visit; perhaps by summer her father would relent, or more likely, she would think of some other scheme for winning her freedom. For now, she was too tired to make plans.

"I am so glad you will stay with us!" said Aunt Phoebe, clapping her hands. "We will make sure your time here is pleasant. You can sketch, and read with us, and enjoy the garden, and . . . oh dear, it all sounds a bit tame, doesn't it?"

"Of course it does," said Aunt Matilda. "However, I do not at all agree with the duke's instructions regarding Catherine. They seem calculated to goad her into rebellion. I believe it will be best if she is allowed some outdoor exercise and the pleasure of respectable society."

She paused, looking thoughtful. "However, I think our friends here would be quite in a flutter if they knew there was a daughter of a duke in our midst. The word might spread, and if the duke were to find out, it could be quite unpleasant. Will you agree to continue to go by the name Miss Arndale, Catherine?"

Catherine nodded, thinking it was of no consequence. Although grateful to her great-aunts for their concern, she found it impossible to be excited by their well-meant plans for her entertainment. It was unlikely that she would meet any kindred spirits here, and even less likely that Grimsby and Leach would allow her father's decrees to be overturned.

Then Catherine heard a commotion at the front door. The raised voices of Grimsby and Leach, and among them, the deep baritone accents of Mr. Philip Woodmere.

* * *

"I repeat, we are here to visit our friends and their niece," said Philip, trying to curb his impatience with the two dolts before him. "We wish to thank Miss Arndale again for the assistance she gave us this morning, and assure ourselves that she has taken no ill from it."

"She ain't wishful to see no one," said the dour-faced woman. "She don't want nuthin' to do with the loikes of you lot."

Cousin Dorothea looked affronted and frightened at the same time, if that was possible. Philip felt his own temper rising. Was the mysterious young lady truly denying their acquaintance, or was there something more sinister going on here? He didn't know which made him angrier.

"Shush, Grimsby! They hain't supposed to know," said the rough-looking manservant to the woman in a hoarse whisper that Philip had no trouble following.

Know what? he wondered.

The oaf turned back to Philip and Cousin Dorothea and said with a ludicrous attempt at dignity, "The lidies hain't receivin'."

Philip stared at him for a moment in shock. The Arndale sisters always welcomed visitors. This was seriously alarming.

"They *will* see us," he said. Ignoring Cousin Dorothea's incoherent protest, he advanced purposefully upon the man, preparing to thrust him aside. Before he was obliged to carry out his threat, he heard the raised voice of the elder Miss Arndale.

"Leach, Grimsby, you forget yourselves!"

A moment later she appeared in the doorway, behind the ruffian and his female cohort. "Stand aside and let our friends in, or it will be the worse for you!"

The strange pair slunk away, muttering under their breaths. Miss Arndale turned toward Philip and his cousin, with a visible effort to reassume her dignity.

"You must forgive us," she said. "I am afraid my niece's servants are a trifle too protective. Do come in."

Relieved but still curious, Philip followed Miss Arndale to the left, toward the cottage's small, comfortably furnished sitting room. There he saw Miss Phoebe Arndale, and sitting beside her, the mysterious beauty who had saved Lizzie.

He expelled a sigh of relief. He hadn't realized how concerned he'd been for her safety. Thank God she seemed none the worse for her morning's adventure. Seeing the lovely color in her cheeks, he found it more and more difficult to believe she was an invalid.

She looked up, and their eyes met. For a brief instant, he could have sworn she was glad to see him again, then she lowered her gaze and her expression became curiously guarded. He wondered why.

He forced himself to concentrate as the elder Miss Arndale made the necessary introductions and motioned him and his cousin toward a settee.

"Mr. Woodmere, you have already met my niece's daughter, Catherine. Catherine, this is Mr. Woodmere's cousin, Miss Dorothea Woodmere."

Catherine. Philip mentally savored the sound of her name, wishing it were proper for him to use it. That he could be alone with her and try to persuade her to confide her troubles to him. However, that was impossible, given their three chaperones.

"We wish to thank you again for saving Lizzie," he said politely.

She looked back at him then. She blushed slightly, and made a little deprecating gesture with her hand. An elegant, long-fingered hand, strong and graceful like the rest of her.

"How is she?" she asked in a friendlier tone than he'd heard from her before.

"Happily plotting her next escapade, no doubt," he replied.

She gave a little laugh. He loved the musical sound of her low-pitched voice.

"We got her home and dry quickly enough," he continued. "I do not believe she will take ill from it. I trust *you've* taken no harm from your wetting?"

"None at all."

"Are you making a long stay here?" asked Cousin Dorothea.

"At—at least a few months, I think," said Miss Arndale. Philip wondered at her hesitation. He looked at her great-aunts, and saw that they looked faintly uncomfortable as well.

"We hope dear Catherine will be able to stay with us until the summer, at least," added Miss Phoebe after a pause.

"We have heard you are here for your health, Miss Arndale," said Cousin Dorothea. "I trust it is no infectious complaint?"

Philip winced at his cousin's words. She sounded rude and prying. However, he couldn't deny that he wanted to know the answer as well.

Miss Catherine Arndale seemed strangely at a loss for an answer.

Her elder great-aunt replied for her. "The noise and

crowds of London were trying to Catherine's nerves. She has come here for peace and quiet, and healthful exercise."

Philip thought there was something studied in Miss Matilda's manner as she gave the explanation. However, his cousin was clearly delighted.

"Oh, so you come from London!" she exclaimed. "I thought your dress was in the very latest mode. Well, I trust you will feel up to partaking in our local society."

"Of course," said Miss Phoebe. "Catherine is most eager to meet all our dear friends."

He looked at Miss Catherine to see her reaction, and realized she had been looking at him. She averted her gaze, but not before he got the impression that she was less than eager at the prospect. Did she think herself above her company? Why?

He directed a meaningful glance at his cousin, to remind her of what they'd planned earlier. With relief, he noted the comprehension in her eyes.

"Perhaps you will all do us the honor of coming to a dinner party this coming Thursday?" she asked.

The older Miss Arndales accepted eagerly. For the rest of the visit his cousin pelted the younger Miss Arndale with a multitude of questions about the latest *on-dits* from London. She answered politely but uncommunicatively,

Perhaps she was merely annoyed by Cousin Dorothea's incessant questions. However, there was definitely something guarded in her manner, which was perfectly proper and even demure. She didn't seem at all like the brave young Amazon who had leaped into the stream to save Lizzie, nor like the imperious lady who had scolded him so fiercely by its banks.

He'd come hoping to learn more of her, but now he had even more questions than before.

On the way home, Cousin Dorothea chattered continuously about the young Miss Arndale, complaining about her reticence and wondering why she put on such airs. Out of habit, he lent his cousin only half an ear, although he, too, was pondering the riddle of the new lady at Larkspur Cottage.

Try as he would, he could come up with no satisfactory explanation for her presence, or for the strange behavior of her servants. Perhaps she'd been sent here to weather out some scandal or a blighted romance. She might even be increasing. He recoiled at the thought, then forced himself to face the possibility. Although she showed no signs of pregnancy, it might be the early days.

He knew so little about her. The only certainty was that however distressing the knowledge might be he had to know more.

Catherine watched Mr. Woodmere and his garrulous cousin leave with a sense of relief. It had been a strain to answer Miss Woodmere's questions. Mr. Woodmere had said little, but several times she had noticed his gaze linger on her.

She had struggled not to stare back, or show any other signs of self-consciousness. Hopefully she had succeeded. Aunt Phoebe and Aunt Matilda would surely be shocked and horrified if they knew her thoughts, as would Mr. Woodmere himself.

She reminded herself again that he was not a handsome man. Nevertheless, he had managed to fill the small room with a strong, virile presence. It was quite unfair that such a respectable gentleman should put her so strongly in mind of the Corsair. There were the "dark eyebrows" and "sable curls," the swarthy complexion and rugged physique. And eyes like molten mahogany.

Of course, there was no "laughing devil in his sneer," she made haste to remind herself. Mr. Woodmere's smile and his manners were totally conventional and nothing at all out of the ordinary. She *did* like the timbre of his voice. Unbidden, another phrase from Byron came to mind—"his deep yet tender melody of tone . . ."

"So what did you think of our dear Mr. Woodmere?"

Catherine started, and stared at Aunt Phoebe.

"I was hoping that making a new friend might console you for missing your London friends," Aunt Phoebe said brightly.

Catherine could not mistake her meaning. She tried to suppress the color that threatened to flood her cheeks. It seemed Aunt Phoebe wished to match-make. How could she tell her it was ridiculous, without offending her? She certainly couldn't tell her great-aunts what she had just been thinking!

"Don't you start meddling, Phoebe," Aunt Matilda said with a frown at her sister, saving Catherine the necessity of a response. "Have you forgotten that he has been courting Charlotte Maldon?"

"But they are not the least in love, Mattie," said Aunt Phoebe.

"What does that matter? She needs a home, and he needs a sensible wife to help manage his brothers and sisters. They will make a match of it. Besides, the duke would never countenance a match between Catherine and a commoner, excellent person though he is."

Catherine felt oddly disappointed at the story, even though Aunt Matilda's words confirmed her judgment of Mr. Woodmere. An eminently practical man, intent on an eminently sensible match. All the more reason to hide her misplaced attraction to him, and to nip in the bud any admiration he might have for her.

"Do not worry, Aunt Matilda. I do not intend to do anything foolish," she replied.

"Oh, but Mr. Woodmere is *such* a dear," continued Aunt Phoebe, seeming undaunted. "He is always doing the kindest things, like bringing over the loveliest trout and game for our dinner, and sending his carriage to fetch us whenever there is a party. I am sure he will do so on Thursday. He always does."

"Which reminds me," said Aunt Matilda, getting up and going toward the hall. "Leach! Grimsby! Come here at once!" she commanded.

Grimsby and Leach came quickly, but their faces registered a wary belligerence. Leach opened his mouth to speak, but Aunt Matilda forestalled him.

"This morning's escapade has proven that you are both wholly unsuited for the positions the duke hired you," she said.

The pair winced. Catherine could see a trace of apprehension appear on their faces.

Aunt Matilda continued, in the same imperious manner. "I have been sorely tempted to write to His Grace and tell him of your incompetence."

Her measured sentences were having their effect. Both Leach and Grimsby opened their mouths and began to make excuses.

Aunt Matilda held a hand up. "Silence! I will listen

to no excuses. However, you will be relieved to know that I have reconsidered. I will refrain from exposing your folly to the duke, but only upon several conditions."

She paused, presumably for effect. Leach and Grimsby watched her apprehensively.

"I believe my niece's rebelliousness to be largely due to the unreasonable restrictions that have been placed upon her. I must insist that she be allowed to go for walks in the countryside, and that she be permitted to make the acquaintance of our friends in the valley."

"But that's against 'Is Grace's horders, that is," protested Leach.

"What he does not know will not harm him. I *do* know the consequences to both of you if he were to get word that while in a drunken stupor you allowed his daughter to escape out of an upper-story window, and nearly drown in a stream! You have your choice."

Catherine watched Aunt Matilda in awestruck admiration. Leach and Grimsby were clearly wavering.

"Well, it seems we ain't got no choice," Grimsby muttered.

Leach looked back at Grimsby, then at Aunt Matilda. Reluctantly, he nodded.

Aunt Matilda gave them an arctic smile. "I am glad you have decided to see reason. Now, since my niece has given her word that she will not try to run away, your services as guards will no longer be needed. Instead, *you*," she said, looking at Leach, "will make yourself useful, tending the fires and helping in the garden. And as for *you*," she said, looking at Grimsby, "you will learn your duties as a ladies' maid. You shall learn how to dress my niece's hair properly, and how to care for her clothing. Can you sew?"

Grimsby gave a doubtful nod. Aunt Matilda went on giving orders to the bemused couple, and Catherine congratulated herself on having remained silent. Aunt Matilda was more than formidable; if the war against Bonaparte had not been over Catherine would have suggested she join Wellington's staff.

Later that evening, Catherine lay in bed, pondering how she might eventually regain her freedom. However, her thoughts were muddled, perhaps due to the sound of Grimsby and Leach in the kitchen below, grumbling about their lot, and about the frightful silence of the countryside. Catherine was more than a little amused; no doubt to those who had spent all their lives in London, the blessed peace of a mountain vale did seem deathly quiet.

Grimsby and Leach finally stopped talking, and Catherine could savor the silence of the night. She had left her window open a crack, relishing the fresh though chilly air. Now, as she lay surprisingly awake, she heard strange rushings and gurglings in the distance. She realized she was hearing the sound of several torrents and waterfalls, what Aunt Phoebe had told her were locally called *forces,* that came down nearby mountainsides. She found it surprisingly soothing.

She wondered that she was not more distressed by the failure of today's attempt to escape. But then, she had always known that she had not so much longed to run away *with* Verwood, as to run away *from* her father, stepmother, and the rest of them. At least she was no longer in the ducal household. Moreover, Aunt Matilda, God bless her, had drastically improved the conditions of her exile. Now she might at least get a chance to see some of this district, renowned for its natural beauties.

However, she would have to tread warily in local society. For her great-aunts' sake, she would have to pretend to be their well-behaved niece, Miss Catherine Arndale. Pray she didn't betray their kindness by some stupid mistake. She could see Mr. Woodmere was already suspicious.

She tossed restlessly for a while, trying not to think about how she had felt when he had put his arms around her to steady her on the banks of the stream, or when he had gazed at her with those candidly admiring brown eyes.

Finally, the music of the forces lulled her to sleep.

Five

The next morning, Catherine arose early, greeted again by the sound of birds outside her window. After a hearty breakfast with her great-aunts, she went for her first ramble about the local countryside. On their advice, she took a path up one of the hills on the southern rim of the valley, to a spot that gave a view of Ullswater.

Grimsby and Leach accompanied her, obviously still thinking she might attempt an escape from the valley. They made no secret of their dissatisfaction with the steepness of the path, or the aching of their feet, but Catherine was not about to allow their complaints to dim her enjoyment. She was swifter than either of them, and soon left the pair far below her. Enjoying a brief spell of freedom, she climbed to the crest of the hill. She felt a keen delight in her first view of the lake, its surface sparkling with waves, its sinuous lines bordered with varied woodlands, sporting the pale and luminous greens of springtime alongside the darker shades of evergreens.

On her return to Larkspur Cottage, she worked with her aunts in their garden, and read with them in the evening. The next few days fell into the same pleasant pattern. She continued to enjoy her walks, and found the company of her aunts much less tiresome than her father had led her to expect. Aunt Phoebe shared her taste for poetry, and Aunt Matilda's astute and caustic observations on the events reported in the *Morning Post* (kindly provided to them by Mr. Woodmere) were wryly amusing. Still, she missed her pianoforte and her friends. She also felt restless and adrift; she had not been able to think of a plan to achieve a permanent freedom that would not dangerously distress Aunt Phoebe.

Several times she saw Mr. Woodmere out and about, walking or riding a sturdy-looking black horse. He always greeted her cordially, but with Grimsby and Leach guarding her like dogs no further conversation was possible. She told herself this was no loss. He certainly would not enter into her feelings about the local scenery. Natives of a such a district usually were indifferent to the beauty of their surroundings. He was a country squire; no doubt his conversation would all be of sheep and turnips.

On the fourth day after her arrival at Larkspur Cottage, Catherine set off for her customary walk. At random, she chose a path she had not taken before, one that led up through a wooded hillside toward a low peak on the east end of the vale. This time only Grimsby accompanied her, Aunt Mattie having set Leach to some task in the garden.

Deliberately, Catherine set a splitting pace up the hillside. As she had hoped, Grimsby soon lagged far behind. Catherine continued to follow the path, which went fairly straight up through the woods until rather suddenly she was out in the open, on a high flat meadow at the crown of the hill. A breeze caught at her bonnet, and she turned so she could feel it on her face.

Then she saw it. A perfect, beautifully arranged circle of stones, like Stonehenge, but in miniature, for the highest of the stones seemed barely three or four feet high. No wonder it was not visible from below the woods that encircled the hill.

She caught her breath at the beauty of the spot. From this hilltop, crowned by the stone circle, she could see for miles around. Below her she could see the road leading into the valley, and the stream meandering down from the fells at the opposite end. All around, high peaks rose, shading to blue-green in the distance. Ullswater glittered off to the south. Overhead, a hawk soared in broad, lofty circles.

It was glorious. Catherine wished her friends could be here to share in her pleasure. Penelope in particular would love to sketch this place.

Looking back toward the woods, Catherine reckoned that it would take Grimsby at least another twenty minutes to catch up with her. Twenty minutes of solitude to enjoy before Grimsby arrived to complain about her corns and plague her to return to the cottage.

Catherine walked around the entire ring, then sat down on one end of a long, flat stone lying just outside it. She leaned back and lost herself in contemplation of the hawk's flight, and of the shifting patterns of light and dark made by clouds scudding over the surrounding hilltops.

How far she was from the duke, the duchess, and Lady Susannah! Here, for a few blessed moments, there was no one to scrutinize her, no servant ready to bear tales against her. She rose from the stone, stretched her arms out wide, and whirled around in a wild dance at the sheer joy of it.

"Miss Arndale?"

She stopped spinning, and saw Mr. Woodmere just a few yards away. He was gazing at her intently with those mahogany eyes; the breeze ruffled his waving dark hair. At first it seemed almost as if he had appeared by some magical conjuration. Then she noticed another path coming out from the woods, from the direction of his home. Of course, he must have come that way.

And seen her dancing like a madwoman!

Blushing, she bade him good morning with all the dignity she could muster.

"Good morning," he echoed. "What do you think of my little Druidical temple?"

"*Your* temple?" she asked, thrown back into her earlier confusion.

"Well, it is on my land," he said, a gleam of humor in his eyes. "I discovered it as a lad. The entire hill was wooded then. Many of the stones were hidden under the overgrowth, and some had fallen over. My father had an interest in antiquities, so he had the hilltop cleared, and righted the stones that had fallen. Now we make sure sheep graze here often, so that the ring might remain open to the skies."

"I am so glad," she said.

"Some of the local people dread the place, calling it frightening and heathenish, but I've never found it so."

"Oh no," she said. "I do not know what gods the Druids worshipped, but surely one feels closer to any divine presence in such a sublime setting."

"I feel that, too," he said, smiling at her. "May I join you?" he added, gesturing toward the oblong stone on which she had sat herself.

She nodded. It would be rude to do otherwise, and yet she felt suddenly uneasy. With just a few words and a warm smile, he had shattered the image she had made of him as an unrefined country squire.

Now he was more dangerously attractive than ever.

Her pulses began to jump at his proximity next to her on the stone seat. She reminded herself that he was a respectable gentleman, all but engaged to the equally respectable Miss Maldon. It would be a disaster to develop a *tendre* for him.

"What troubles you, Miss Arndale?" he asked.

She glanced at him, then looked away, surprised at the depth of concern she heard in his voice and read in his face. What could she say?

"Forgive me for prying," he continued. "But something *is* distressing you. I only wish to know if there is any way that I can help."

She struggled to decide how to answer him. Perhaps his offer was prompted by gratitude for what she had done for his sister, but it was kind of him nonetheless. It would be rude to repulse his offer, but what could she tell him? She could not break her promise to her great-aunts by revealing her identity or relating the scandalous circumstances behind her presence here.

"It is understandable you should be curious," she said finally, choosing her words with care. "There are so many strange circumstances surrounding my arrival here. But I am afraid I cannot explain them to you."

He looked down, his expression thoughtful. She knew he was disappointed, but what could she do?

"There are reasons why my family has sent me here," she continued. "I can only assure you I have never intentionally harmed anyone. Nor do I intend anything but good toward my aunts and their friends."

He looked back at her, searching her face with his gaze.

"Do you believe me?" she asked, unsure why it was so important that he did.

"I believe you."

His reply was firm, but his expression was still grave. It troubled Catherine somehow. Then she realized she had a deeper reason for not wanting to confide in him: a strong but foolish desire to have him think well of her.

Then she heard Grimsby's rasping breath behind them. Turning, she saw the woman a few dozen yards away, coming out of the woods. She saw that Mr. Woodmere had heard Grimsby as well. He looked disappointed that their encounter was over, but Catherine told herself she was glad.

"Good-bye," she said, getting up from the stone seat.

"Good-bye, Miss Arndale," he said, following suit. "Don't forget that if there is ever anything I can do for you, you have only to let me know."

She thanked him, and turned to meet Grimsby, who was watching Mr. Woodmere with a suspicious eye. However, Grimsby seemed too winded to say much, nor did she scold Catherine on the way back to the cottage. Catherine was glad of her silence; she was disinclined to talk, feeling more disturbed by her encounter with Mr. Woodmere than she wanted to admit.

She had known a strong impulse to confide in him. She hated having to lie to him, but even more so, she dreaded having him discover the truth.

Suddenly she longed for her friends. Juliana and Penelope would never turn their backs upon her. She wished she could write to them, but Aunt Matilda had reluctantly forbidden it, fearing they might alert Verwood to her direction. Catherine couldn't help wondering how her friends were faring. Were they still as unhappy as she'd left them? Did they think she'd forgotten them?

"It's been almost two weeks, Jule. Should we have received a letter from Catherine by now?"

Penelope looked anxiously at Juliana, strolling beside her down the Queen's Walk in Green Park.

"Yes, we should have," Juliana replied, glancing behind them to make sure their maids were still at a discreet distance.

They strolled together in silence for a few moments. Pen usually enjoyed her morning walks with Juliana, especially here where she could imagine herself back in the country. Now, however, her pleasure was clouded by thoughts of what might have befallen Catherine. Juliana's thoughtful expression hinted that she shared Pen's worries.

"Why haven't we heard, then?" she asked. "Please tell me I am being foolish. I keep imagining the most dreadful things. Do you think perhaps she has just been too busy to write?"

Juliana shook her head with obvious reluctance. "You know Cat always keeps her promises. If she had gotten away safely with Verwood, she would have written."

Penelope could not deny it. "What do you think has happened, then?"

"I don't know. Perhaps the duke got wind of the elopement, and stopped them somehow. Perhaps he has sent Catherine off somewhere in disgrace."

"Oh, I do hope that is what happened!"

"You hope so? What could possibly be worse?"

"I fear—oh, it is the most horrible thought! Perhaps—perhaps Lord Verwood never truly meant to marry Catherine, and now he has deserted her somewhere."

Juliana frowned. "Cat seemed so sure he would not betray her. Let's not think the worst until we know for certain."

Her tone was bracing, but Pen could see Jule shared her fears.

"I wish we did know for certain. If she is in some sort of trouble, perhaps there is something we could do to help."

"Well, I cannot bear to keep waiting like this," said Juliana, lengthening her stride.

"What do you think we should do?" asked Pen, doing her best to keep up.

"Find out for ourselves."

Later that day, Juliana's barouche bore her and Penelope toward the Whitgrave mansion. She had convinced Mrs. Frisby, the widowed lady Grandpapa had hired to be her companion, that she and Penelope were merely going shopping. No doubt Mrs. Frisby would have palpitations if she knew what Juliana and Pen were actually planning to do.

Juliana took a deep breath as they turned into Berkeley Square. She tried to steel herself for what was likely to be a most unpleasant encounter. She could see Pen was even more apprehensive.

"Do you think they will receive us?" asked

Penelope, her face even paler than usual under its dusting of freckles.

"I hope so," she replied. "Courage, Pen. Remember, it's all for Catherine's sake."

Pen nodded, though she still looked frightened. Together, they dismounted from the carriage and climbed the steps toward the colonnaded entrance to Whitgrave House. Juliana knocked on the door, which was opened by a portly butler.

Lifting her chin, Juliana stepped forward, saying, "I am Miss Hutton, and this is my friend, Miss Talcott. We are friends of Lady Catherine, and we are come to inquire after her health."

"It is not my place to satisfy your curiosity," said the butler, his voice clearly calculated to mortify them.

Juliana tried to ignore her annoyance at his manner. "May we speak to Her Grace the duchess, then?"

"Her Grace is not receiving visitors today."

"I have heard that she is," said Juliana. "We *will* see her."

"You will leave now. I regret to inform you that His Grace has given orders you are not to be received here."

"I regret to inform you I am indifferent to His Grace's orders!" she said, and swept past him.

He turned to gape at her, shock written all over his face. Quickly, Juliana ran across the marble floor and mounted the stairs, gesturing to Penelope to follow. They heard the butler call out, presumably to the footmen, then they heard footsteps behind them. Juliana wondered for a moment if she and Penelope were going to be forcibly ejected. However, they reached the landing without being overtaken. Running past a startled footman, they entered the first room they saw.

Juliana paused on the threshold, temporarily dazzled by the light reflected from several gilt mirrors hanging on the walls opposite the windows. More gilding covered the elaborately carved doorways, the moldings, and even the ceiling of the room, contrasting brightly against the red walls. Amid this sumptuous splendor sat the duchess, along with her daughter and several other female visitors. The duchess scowled as she saw Juliana and Penelope in the doorway.

"What is the meaning of this?" she asked imperiously. Juliana turned her head, and saw that both the butler and the footman had followed them into the room. "Send these young persons away immediately!"

"They persisted, Your Grace!" the butler said breathlessly, stepping in front of Juliana. "They thrust me aside—I could not stop them. I assure you I will not permit such an outrage—"

Juliana felt as if she had been slapped, but she had not come this far to give up so easily. She stepped around the butler and faced the duchess's supercilious gaze with a determined one of her own.

"We are here to inquire after Lady Catherine's health," she said, lifting her chin.

The duchess glanced briefly toward the other women in the room, who were all watching curiously. Juliana could see she was trying to decide whether she could best avoid a scene by allowing them to stay, or by refusing to speak with them.

"Very well, I will speak with you," she said. "Butterford, you may go."

As the butler and footman left the room, the duchess turned back to Juliana and Penelope. She made no attempt to introduce them to the other ladies, nor to offer them a seat. Juliana knew it was deliberate.

"Lady Catherine is suffering from an irritation of the nerves, brought on by the exigencies of the Season," the duchess announced, in a manner that Juliana suspected had been carefully rehearsed. "His Grace and I are convinced that she will do better to live secluded in the country, and protected from *unsuitable* influences."

Juliana winced inwardly at the not-too subtle reference to herself and Penelope. She could see Catherine's sister, Lady Susannah, barely hiding her delight at their discomfiture and her triumph at Catherine's banishment. And no wonder, thought Juliana. Lady Susannah had probably always been jealous of Catherine.

Juliana clenched her hands in an attempt to control her anger, until she felt her nails digging into her palms. She reminded herself that she and Pen were there to find out what had happened to Catherine, and forced herself to analyze what the duchess had said. Unfortunately, Her Grace's face was cold and impassive, and Juliana was not sure what to make of it. She might be covering up for Catherine's elopement, or perhaps she and the duke really had sent Catherine off somewhere.

"How—how kind of you, Your Grace," said Penelope, as Juliana was still trying to think of a response. Pen continued in her sweetest voice. "May we have her direction so that we may write to her?"

Pen's voice quavered a little, but she was looking the duchess in the eye. Juliana knew Pen was not so naive as to think the duchess would help them; this must be her way of challenging Her Grace's story in the most unexceptionable manner possible.

Bravo, Pen! thought Juliana, seeing Her Grace at a

temporary loss. It seemed she really was trying to hide something. A moment later, however, the duchess seemed to regain her aplomb.

"Of course you may write to her," she said with a smile that Juliana did not trust for an instant. "I do not have the direction to hand, but if you send your letters here, I assure you we will send them on to Lady Catherine in good time."

Juliana and Penelope exchanged glances. Juliana could see that Pen shared her skepticism. No letter from either of them would ever reach Cat through the duke or duchess. Unfortunately, it still was not clear whether Her Grace actually knew Catherine's whereabouts.

For a moment, Juliana toyed with the notion of challenging the story, but rejected it. She would only destroy Cat's reputation if she spoke of her attempted elopement in front of the other ladies.

"Thank you, Your Grace," she said, the words sticking in her throat. "Good day."

Penelope nervously echoed her words, and they left the room. As they went down the stairs, they could hear the assembled ladies discussing their intrusion. "Such effrontery . . . intolerable mushrooms . . ."

Juliana could not breathe easily until she and Penelope made themselves comfortable again in the barouche. She had been called a mushroom before, but it was no more pleasant the twentieth time than the first. She hated having had to do this, as much as she hated the fact that her grandfather wanted to continuously thrust her into such situations, where she was sure to be snubbed. She would never belong to this world, would never be happy in it.

She thrust her selfish thoughts aside. Even though

the visit had not yielded any useful information, she could not regret having tried, for Catherine's sake.

She turned to Penelope, whose face mirrored her own frustration.

"So what do you think?" she asked, quietly so that the coachman would not overhear.

"I think the duchess is hiding something."

"She could be just covering up for the elopement, I suppose," mused Juliana. "Perhaps they are going to pretend it was just a quiet wedding in the country, rather than have it be known that Catherine ran away from them."

"I don't know. I am afraid it is something worse."

"Do you still think Verwood might have run away with her and abandoned her? And that they are trying to cover it up?"

Pen nodded, eyes wide with concern.

"I suppose that might be possible," Juliana replied. "I am going to try to find some way to discover the truth. Until we do, we should not imagine the worst. In fact," she continued, trying to reassure herself as well as Penelope, "I think it would be just like the duke to pack Cat off somewhere with some dreadfully dull relations. I would wager she is perfectly well, just bored to tears!"

Six

"Have I got it right, me lady?"

Catherine turned her head and smiled up at Grimsby, who had just laboriously put the final pins in Catherine's hair.

"Yes, it is very well done indeed," she said, amused to see the hint of an unaccustomed smile pass over Grimsby's face. Over the past week, both Grimsby and Leach had made earnest efforts to learn their newly appointed tasks. No doubt they were coming to realize that despite all the hills they had to climb, their lot here was actually far easier and more pleasant than their previous lives in London.

Catherine looked back at her reflection in the small mirror and was more than satisfied that she was properly attired for the dinner party at Woodmere Hall. She had chosen a gown she had worn last Season, an ice blue muslin, simple and demure, and the plainest of the jewelry in her trinket box: a pair of silver earrings and a matching locket, containing strands of her own hair entwined with some of Juliana's and Penelope's. It was just as well she hadn't any of her more costly jewelry; it would have been quite out of place on simple Miss Catherine Arndale of Larkspur Cottage.

She chuckled, thinking of how shocked her stepmother and stepsister would be at her transformation.

They always reveled in the attention their rank brought, and would never understand that Catherine sometimes found it irksome.

"Me lady?" asked Grimsby. "Is something wrong?"

"Nothing, Grimsby. You have done a fine job," she replied as she got up from her chair.

In truth, she found herself looking forward to dining at Woodmere Hall with quite a foolish degree of anticipation. Her great-aunts were excited at the prospect of introducing her to their friends, and she reminded herself how important it was not to disappoint them by behaving in any way that might put to the blush. That included making sure she did not show any improper interest in the master of Woodmere Hall.

She thanked Grimsby, and went downstairs where Aunt Matilda and Aunt Phoebe awaited her, the former in a stiff black bombazine and the latter in pale green satin trimmed with lace. Aunt Phoebe clapped her hands excitedly, and Aunt Matilda calmly complimented Catherine on her appearance.

"We have had delightful news," said Aunt Phoebe. "Frank Maldon—that is, *Captain* Maldon, has come to visit. Sir George's younger brother, you know, and his heir, too. He last visited several years ago, but Lady Maldon says that now that he has made his fortune in the navy he is looking to settle nearby."

Catherine merely smiled at Aunt Phoebe's renewed attempt at matchmaking. A few minutes later, they all went out toward the awaiting carriage sent by Mr. Woodmere.

Less than fifteen minutes' drive brought them to within sight of Woodmere Hall. Built on a rise on the side of the valley, backed by rugged hilltops, it was a substantial but simply designed building, of local blue-gray stone. A peel tower at one corner lent it a vaguely medieval air. According to Aunt Matilda, such towers had been built in less peaceful times, to guard against invasion from the north.

In a less grand setting, the stark design and the corner tower might have looked forbidding, but Catherine decided that the house perfectly suited its surroundings. Softened by plantings of old oak trees and drifts of daffodils, with lights shining through its lower story windows, it seemed both protective and welcoming, as if it were willing and happy to shelter its owners and their guests against inclement winds.

Once inside, the impression of comfort only increased. As a respectable-looking butler led them through the house, Catherine took in the stone floors and the massive oak furniture, some of which looked ancient but all gleaming with beeswax. There were a number of pictures on the walls, including portraits and landscapes, executed with varying degrees of artistry, but tastefully arranged.

Catherine would have liked to stop and study some of the paintings. Instead, she dutifully followed her great-aunts into a drawing room decorated in warm, deep shades of gold, burgundy, and emerald, where the Woodmeres and a small crowd of guests were sitting and conversing near the large fire. Mr. Woodmere arose quickly and came forward to greet them, closely followed by his sister and cousin.

He looked so well in his evening garb that Catherine was obliged to remind herself again that he was not a handsome man. Not at all! It was just that his snowy white shirt and well-cut black coat heightened the impact of his swarthy complexion and dark locks. Still, she wasn't sure he did not look his best as she had first seen him, in his shirtsleeves and buckskins, and struggled to suppress the memory.

When their eyes met, she saw a warmth in his that alerted her to a new danger. It seemed he might be developing feelings for her besides gratitude. Determined not to give him any encouragement, she looked past him, only to catch her breath at another tantalizing sight.

In a corner of the spacious room she saw the beautiful curves and artfully turned legs of a Broadwood grand! She hadn't imagined that anyone in this valley would own such a magnificent instrument. Apparently Mr. Woodmere was a very well-to-do gentleman farmer. But was the lovely pianoforte a mere pretension, or did someone actually play? She struggled to suppress the urge to go over and see if it was in tune.

Her host noticed the direction of her gaze and asked, "Do you play, Miss Arndale?"

"A little," she replied. Modestly, as befit Miss Catherine Arndale of Larkspur Cottage.

"Perhaps you will play for us later, then," he said.

Heart leaping at the prospect, Catherine had to force herself to pay attention and smile as Miss Woodmere introduced the other guests.

Sir George Maldon, a red-faced portly gentleman who looked to be in his early forties, gave her a jovial smile, but his wife Amelia, Lady Maldon, who seemed very conscious of her position as the ranking lady of the district, gave Catherine a minimal, condescending nod. Catherine smiled politely back at Lady Maldon, repressing a chuckle at the thought of how Lady Maldon would feel if she knew she had just slighted a duke's daughter.

Next, Catherine met the Dowager Lady Maldon,

who she understood to be the present baronet's cousin, and her daughter Charlotte, the lady Mr. Woodmere was reputedly courting. A quiet young woman in a sober brown dress, Miss Maldon did not present the joyful appearance of a lady being courted by the gentleman of her choice.

Catherine briefly worried that perhaps *she* was the cause of Miss Maldon's unhappiness, but then her attention was sought by Captain Maldon, Sir George's brother and heir. She found Aunt Phoebe had not exaggerated his charm; Captain Maldon was not only tall and fair-haired, but he had quite an engaging smile. He paid Catherine a few compliments, but she was experienced enough to see that he had only flirtation in mind.

Next, she was introduced to the vicar and his wife, who seemed a kindly couple, and to the Cotterfields. Mr. and Mrs. Cotterfield were kindly, old-fashioned looking persons, he in a powdered wig, and she in an odd, hooped gown in the fashion of at least thirty years ago. Their offspring, two sons and two daughters, seemed a jolly group.

The Miss Cotterfields, clearly thrilled to learn that she had come from London, plied her with eager questions about the latest fashions, about the city and its diversions. Catherine did her best to answer them, finding their artless friendliness refreshing. In London most ladies had regarded Catherine as a rival. She knew that despite showing her the outward respect that her rank commanded, they gossiped behind her back, and had secretly hoped for her scandalous downfall.

Really, it was rather fun to be Miss Catherine Arndale of Larkspur Cottage!

Nevertheless, her comfort was disturbed by the

awareness that her host was watching her quietly throughout. He was clearly curious about her, and now she feared he might be attracted to her as well. Her unease only increased at the dinner table, where she found herself seated to one side of him. Fortunately, the party was not formal, so she was not obliged to converse only with him.

There were other challenges to face, however. They had just barely been seated when Lady Maldon began inquiring into Catherine's background.

"Miss Catherine, from which part of the country does your family hail?" was her first question.

Catherine had come prepared for this. "From Derbyshire, ma'am," she replied, reflecting that it was a large enough county.

"My eldest sister Jane has settled there," said Mr. Woodmere. "She has married the vicar of Little Hayfield, not far from Whitgrave Castle."

"A—a lovely area of the country," she said, hoping no one had noticed her involuntary reaction to the mention of her family's estate. "Of course, nothing to compare to what one can see *here*."

"I am glad you have found pleasure walking in our valley," said Mr. Woodmere. Simple words, but the smile that accompanied them made Catherine all too aware of his proximity. Just a few inches closer, and their knees might brush under the table, she thought, making sure she sat properly still.

He continued to smile at her, and it was easy enough to see that he admired her. Disastrous! She could not come between him and poor Miss Maldon, seated further down the table. She cast about in her mind for means of dampening his interest. She had been warned that gentlemen were put off by bluestockings; perhaps a decent display of erudition would do the trick.

"Why, I have always wanted to visit the Lakes," she said, and in her most enthusiastic voice, began to recite. " 'Far from my dearest Friend, 'tis mine to rove, through bare grey dell, high wood, and pastoral cove; where Derwent rests, and listens to the roar that stuns the tremulous cliffs of high Lodore.' "

She looked at Mr. Woodmere, fully expecting to see boredom written all over his face.

Instead, he turned toward her, an amused look in his eyes, almost as if he had guessed at her game.

" 'Where peace to Grasmere's lonely island leads, to willowy hedgerows, and to emerald meads,' " he intoned, his deep voice like the richest hot chocolate. " 'Leads to her bridge, rude church, and cottaged grounds, her rocky sheepwalks, and her woodland bounds; where, undisturbed by winds, Winander sleeps 'mid clustering isles, and holly-sprinkled steeps; where twilight glens endear my Esthwaite's shore, and memory of departed pleasures, more.' "

Catherine stifled a gasp and averted her gaze. Perhaps she should have expected this, after their encounter on the hilltop, but who would have guessed that this rustic gentleman would quote Wordsworth? And in a rich, deep voice that made her feel as if she were melting inwardly!

"For God's sake let's not go on with any demmed poetry," said Sir Maldon, conveniently drawing attention away from her. "At least not until I've finished my dinner!"

"Oh, but are we not blessed to live in a place that has inspired so much poetry?" asked the vicar's wife.

"I so agree," said Aunt Phoebe, eyes sparkling.

"Just fancy, Catherine. Mr. Wordsworth was inspired to write those lovely verses on the daffodils just a few miles from here!"

"I know the critics did not care for it, but I for one thought the poem quite charming," replied the vicar's wife.

Muttering, Sir Maldon turned his attention back to his fish, while the others engaged in a discussion of various poems and nearby beauty spots that had inspired them. For the most part, Catherine remained silent, but she could not help but be pleased when an expedition was proposed to Gowbarrow Park, the site of the daffodils in Mr. Wordsworth's poem.

When she and the other ladies returned to the drawing room, she was surprised and delighted to see Lizzie awaiting them there, accompanied by a nursemaid. The little girl's brown eyes, so like her brother's, lit up as she jumped up from her stool and ran to greet Catherine.

Catherine knelt down and opened her arms, and Lizzie ran in, twining her little arms around Catherine with surprising strength. Catherine found the eager embrace touching. It would be fun to get to know this sweet child better. Still, she didn't know how long she would be here. Perhaps it wasn't wise to let Lizzie become too attached to her, she thought with an unexpected pang of regret.

Miss Maldon and the Miss Cotterfields soon came around Catherine and Lizzie, playing with the latter as they might with a doll. Lizzie, clearly enjoying all the attention, recounted with relish the entire tale of her fall in the stream and her subsequent rescue. The ladies all exclaimed over it, putting Catherine to the blush.

Before long, the elder Miss Woodmere directed the servant to take Lizzie away. Catherine conversed for a while with the other ladies, but with Lizzie gone, she could not help the occasional longing glance at the beautiful pianoforte in the corner. She reminded herself that like Mr. Woodmere, the lovely instrument posed a dangerous temptation. Perhaps it was best that she didn't play.

"Marianne, you must play for us," said Miss Woodmere, as the gentlemen began to enter the room. "It is time to show off that sonatina you have been practicing."

Marianne pouted, looking as surly as such a pretty girl could. Catherine could tell Marianne had not practiced enough, and was therefore reluctant to perform. Then suddenly, Marianne beamed and looked at Catherine.

"Perhaps *you* will play for us," she said. *"Please."*

There was nothing to be done. Catherine smilingly accepted the invitation, and walked over to the pianoforte, forcing herself not to run.

She sat down and played a few scales to limber up her fingers, wishing she were not so out of practice herself. To her utter delight, the instrument *was* in tune. Now what to play?

She was acutely conscious of the curious onlookers, the expectant faces of her aunts, and of Mr. Woodmere. She decided against her beloved Beethoven. She couldn't risk embarrassing herself or her aunts with too great a show of sensibility. Instead, she decided on a lively Mozart sonata and began to play.

Philip listened in amazement. Charlotte was the only lady he knew who could even attempt to play such a piece. Although Charlotte played very well and it was always a pleasure to listen to her, Miss Arndale's playing was something else indeed.

Her long, graceful fingers ran over the keys effortlessly. Even in the fastest passages, each individual note was as clear and brilliant as a star on a cloudless night. He noticed with awe that she never repeated a passage the same way twice. She was not merely using some prearranged, formal embellishments. She was improvising, truly *playing* the instrument, with brilliance, vivacity, and imagination. When she came to the slower, more lyrical middle part of the piece, he closed his eyes, savoring the way she made the pianoforte sing. What would it be like to hear such playing every day?

He caught himself on that thought. How could he think so of a lady he knew so little about? Her facility with the pianoforte was just one more facet of the enigma she presented. Where had she learned to play so? How long must she have practiced to acquire such skill?

Philip tried to remember what the Miss Arndales had said about their family. They'd come to live here many years ago, when their widowed father had taken the position of vicar at Lynthwaite Church. They sometimes spoke of a few relations in Derbyshire, but Philip had always gotten the impression that it was a small family, in quite modest circumstances.

Perhaps Miss Arndale had received extensive education in the feminine accomplishments in preparation for becoming a governess, as Charlotte planned to do. Perhaps that explained her subdued demeanor at dinner. He was sure there was passion behind that demure facade; he'd had a glimpse of it the day they'd talked on Druid's Hill.

There was certainly a restrained passion in the way she played. The slower melody of the second movement had given way to a brilliant finale. Her eyes were bright and her face intense with concentration and a keen joy in the music.

What a waste it would be if she were destined to become a governess! Then he remembered she had two servants, and realized that whatever her trouble was, it could not be poverty. More likely his earlier conjectures were true, that she came from a wealthy family, and had been sent to her great-aunts' isolated home to weather out some scandal. He would be wise not to allow himself to become too enchanted with her.

He didn't want to be wise.

With several bright, spirited chords, Miss Arndale finished the sonata. She looked up and smiled uncertainly, as if unsure of the reception her playing would receive.

He smiled back at her, and their gazes locked. For a moment he thought he saw something in her expression he couldn't define. A lingering look of pleasure in the music she'd made, but something else as well. A yearning, a desire for his approval perhaps?

It made as little sense as the rest.

He might even have been mistaken, for she looked away from him toward the others, returning him to an awareness of his guests. He could see that Sir George had slept through the latter part of the performance. The Philistine! However, most of the others were heartily applauding Miss Arndale's playing. Even Frank Maldon and those irritating Cotterfield lads, who didn't know one note from another, were falling all over themselves to praise her. Philip stifled a spurt of jealousy as he watched her accept their compliments.

She looked both relieved and happier than he'd seen her before, and it now occurred to him that he might be able, in a small way, to repay the debt he owed her for saving Lizzie's life.

"Miss Arndale, you play wonderfully," he said, when the others had finished praising her. "You must be missing your music since your aunts have no instrument. We would be very honored if you would come here and play ours. Every day if you wish."

Her heart was in her eyes then, full of mingled longing and doubt. She looked at her aunts, and both Miss Matilda and Miss Phoebe nodded their approval of the scheme.

He could see from her pursed lips that Cousin Dorothea was less than enamored of the idea. She'd been in a sour mood ever since the governess had left, and in addition, seemed to have taken something of a dislike to Miss Catherine Arndale. He braced himself to deal with her should she make an objection.

"Perhaps you might take over Miss Marianne's music lessons as well, Miss Arndale," she said.

Philip winced at her tone, which implied that Miss Arndale was unwelcome unless she made herself useful.

"Oh, would you?" asked Marianne, looking at Miss Arndale eagerly.

Philip felt torn when he saw the look of hero worship in his sister's face. He'd so wanted her to apply herself to her playing. He'd hoped Marianne would bring music into the house, as his mother once had.

Instead, his sister only complained when exhorted to practice. Now, her admiration for Miss Arndale seemed to be overcoming her rebellion, but it made him uncomfortable as well. Could he be sure Miss Arndale would prove a good influence on his volatile sister?

She'd assured him she meant no harm, and when he looked in her eyes, he believed her. But was he just besotted?

Then again, she might not wish to teach Marianne, he thought, seeing her hesitate before answering his sister.

"I should be delighted to give you lessons," she said finally, smiling at Marianne.

Philip listened to them make arrangements for Marianne's first lesson, and the realization of what he'd offered struck him. He should probably have been more cautious, but now all he felt was a rising excitement at the thought that Miss Arndale was going to be a frequent, perhaps a daily, visitor to their home.

No, he did not want to be wise.

Seven

The very next day, Miss Arndale arrived to play the pianoforte and to give Marianne her first lesson. Philip made sure to be there to greet her, for he did not trust Cousin Dorothea to provide her a proper welcome. After the dinner party she'd complained about his offering Miss Arndale free use of their pianoforte, and he'd realized she resented Miss Arndale in the same way she'd resented his courtship of Charlotte. She knew that once he married, he would no longer need her to watch over his sisters, and clearly didn't trust his assurances that he would continue to provide for her comfort when she left their household.

However, Dorothea comported herself with reasonable politeness. Philip hoped his and Marianne's warmer welcomes to Miss Arndale made up for Dorothea's want of cordiality. Though tempted to stay and listen, he left Miss Arndale and Marianne to themselves. He did not wish to make either self-conscious. Later that evening, Marianne reported she'd enjoyed her lesson, and that Miss Arndale had a completely different method of teaching from the late, unlamented governess.

Philip restrained himself several more days, but then came a rainy day when he decided to spend the afternoon in his study going over his books. He could hear tantalizing snatches of music coming from the opposite end of the house, and decided it might be time to put in an appearance and see how Miss Arndale and his sister were faring.

He came down the hall. More clearly, he could hear voices singing: Marianne, Miss Arndale, and if he was not mistaken, Lizzie as well. The little imp must have escaped Dorothea to join in the music lesson. They were singing some absurd, frivolous tune, all about flowers and springtime. Absurd, frivolous, and totally delightful.

He stopped on the threshold of the drawing room, reluctant to interrupt but longing to catch sight of Miss Arndale with his sisters.

She was sitting next to Marianne at the pianoforte, Lizzie in her lap. Marianne was playing and singing the main melody of the song in a high, sweet soprano. Miss Arndale played a rippling accompaniment and added a subtle harmony in her soft alto voice, and Lizzie warbled along, looking extremely proud of herself.

They were all blissfully unaware that he was watching them, and he was glad of it. He felt inexpressibly warmed by the charming picture, his sisters in their sprigged gowns, ribbons in their hair, Miss Arndale in a simple walking dress that suited her height and her elegant curves. There was an unguarded happiness in her face that he'd glimpsed only once before, when they'd met at the stone circle.

He wished the moment would last, wished Miss Arndale did not have to leave them, not this afternoon, not this summer. How could he feel so for a lady he barely knew, who held some secret that might cause him untold pain? But he could not deny that he did, and the pain would be even greater if she left before he came to know her better.

When they came to the end of the song, more or less together, he applauded heartily. His sisters looked up and smiled at him, but he was disappointed to see the wary look return to Miss Arndale's face.

"Good afternoon, Miss Arndale," he said. "I see you have acquired a second student."

"I am very glad Lizzie has joined us," she replied.

"But tomorrow, you will teach me by myself, won't you?" asked Marianne.

"You will teach me too, won't you, Miss Arndale?" asked Lizzie with her best puppy look in her eyes.

Philip was not surprised to hear Miss Arndale promise to teach both of them individually the very next day.

"Have you forgotten, Miss Catherine? We are all going to see the daffodils tomorrow," said Lizzie. "You'll have to wait another day to teach us both."

"Of course," said Miss Arndale, with a glimmer of laughter in her eyes, her lips curving enticingly.

"Now you must both allow Miss Arndale to play on her own," Philip said gruffly. "I believe she's earned her chance."

He watched his sisters embrace Miss Arndale, and saw a faint line appear between her brows as she embraced them in turn, as if it pained her somehow. As if she were becoming fond of them, and didn't wish to.

He remembered that she'd said she might only stay until the summer. Just a few short months to try to induce her to confide in him. He didn't know what he would do if he failed.

He turned to follow his sisters out of the room, and

was surprised to hear Miss Arndale asking him to remain for a moment. Instantly, he turned back, and saw her get up from the pianoforte and come toward him.

"Mr. Woodmere, you said I should ask if ever I had need of your help," she said nervously. She handed him a folded paper, and said, "Could you please post this for me?"

He took the letter from her, and couldn't help glancing at the direction. It was addressed to a Miss Juliana Hutton, in Russell Square, in London. Somehow he felt relieved to see the letter addressed to a lady. But why would Miss Arndale ask him to post it, unless she didn't wish her great-aunts to know of the letter? This Miss Hutton might be merely helping Miss Arndale to carry on a clandestine correspondence with some gentleman of whom her family disapproved. If so, it would be highly reprehensible for him to aid her. Not to mention that his whole being rebelled at the thought of helping her to another man, he thought, shaken by the strength of his revulsion.

"Mr. Woodmere, I can see you are wondering why I do not post this with my aunts' letters," she said.

"I must know that if I do this, it is in your best interests."

"I understand," she said, meeting his eyes directly. "I will explain. Since I left London rather suddenly, I wish to assure a friend that I am well and happy. She is the daughter of a tradesman, and my father does not approve of our friendship."

Philip wrinkled his brow. Who *was* she that her father objected to such a friend?

"I don't wish to ask Aunt Mattie to post the letter," she continued. "My father would be so angry if he knew. I am sorry I can tell you no more, but I assure you the letter is perfectly innocent. I have not even indicated a direction for a reply."

He looked into her eyes and knew she was telling the truth, or at least part of it.

"Please, do not ask me any more," she said in a low voice. "Will you do this for me?"

"Very well," he said. "I am going to Penrith later. I can post it from there, so your friend will receive it more quickly."

She thanked him, but though he felt warmed by the gratitude he read in her face, Philip prayed again that he was doing the right thing.

The skies were brilliantly blue and clear the morning of the expedition to Gowbarrow Park. As Catherine paced restlessly outside the cottage, awaiting the arrival of the Woodmeres' carriages, she found herself wishing her own feelings were as clear.

Yesterday's brief conversation with Mr. Woodmere had left her in a decidedly anxious state. She had not precisely lied to him, yet she had told him so little of the truth it felt like a deception. She hated the thought of deceiving him.

The more she knew him, the more she was drawn to him, and she could see that the feeling was mutual. But it was just an infatuation; it had to be. He did not know her, or understand the gulf that separated them as clearly as if they were from different worlds. His destiny lay with kind, respectable Charlotte Maldon, who could take care of his family as they deserved.

If she told him the truth about herself, it would undoubtedly shock him out of his misplaced interest in her. But it would also upset Aunt Phoebe, and that was unthinkable.

She was still trying to decide what to do when she saw the two carriages come around the bend. Mr. Woodmere himself drove the landau, his brothers and sisters riding within. Behind it, a coachman drove the Woodmeres' closed carriage.

The younger Woodmeres all greeted her enthusiastically and insisted she ride with them. She didn't have the heart to refuse, so she climbed into the already crowded landau and took Lizzie onto her lap, as her aunts joined the elder Miss Woodmere in the other carriage.

Soon, they were on their way down the lane that led to the main road out of the valley. At first, the children all chattered excitedly about what they were going to see and do. Apparently this was not the first time they'd been to Gowbarrow Park. From them Catherine learned that besides the daffodils, the park boasted several other attractions, including a castle, a waterfall, and a herd of fallow deer.

A brief lull followed, then Lizzie leaned forward and called to her brother, sitting on the box. Mr. Woodmere turned around and smiled at them.

"Philip, will you please sing to us about Robin Hood?"

A slightly embarrassed expression came over his face; Catherine suspected he felt shy about singing in front of her.

"Perhaps your brother is not feeling inclined to sing today," she said to Lizzie.

"Oh no! Philip loves to sing!" said Lizzie innocently.

Catherine was not surprised when just a little more

wheedling convinced Mr. Woodmere to oblige his youngest sister, or to discover that he had a full, rich baritone that suited the old ballad perfectly. After hearing him recite poetry, she should have guessed he would sing like a god!

There was nothing she could do but abandon herself to the enjoyment of Mr. Woodmere's voice as he sang the tale of how Robin Hood entertained the Bishop of Hereford and relieved him of five hundred pounds. Urged by Lizzie, he sang another stirring ballad, and after that, Harry and Jack sang some sailor songs they'd learned from their brother William. The rest of the short trip was whiled away in the same pleasant manner.

Soon they reached the lake, and turned left, the road following closely along the lakeside, with groves of trees all about. Once in the environs of Gowbarrow Park, the carriages halted, and everyone alighted to stroll by the shore and enjoy the sights while awaiting the arrival of the Cotterfields and the Maldons, who also planned to join the group.

Catherine was delighted. Just as in Mr. Wordsworth's poem, the daffodils were in full bloom, their cheerful faces bright against the turf and mossy stones that surrounded them. Unlike the day that Mr. Wordsworth and his sister had walked there some fifteen years previously, the surface of the lake was smooth and calm, showing only the occasional patch of ripples caused by vagrant breezes. Although the trees were not in leaf yet, many showed the pale green haze of budding leaves. In the background, ranges of hills mounted one behind the other, vibrant in the crystal clear air.

However, Catherine soon found herself diverted

from the beauty of the scene by a quite different sort of attraction.

First the younger Woodmeres had all run down to the water's edge to skip stones, Marianne holding Lizzie's hand tightly and protectively. Then Aunt Phoebe, in a blatant fit of matchmaking, convinced Aunt Mattie and Miss Dorothea Woodmere to sit with her in the landau, and suggested Catherine stroll with Mr. Woodmere. She went along, embarrassed but less unwilling than she should have been.

On the other hand, Mr. Woodmere seemed not the least bit discomposed by Aunt Phoebe's machinations. Catherine found herself relaxing as he talked to her of the lake, telling her how each season revealed its varied charms. Entranced, she listened as he described the autumn tints, the russet tones of the bracken, and the gold of the birches, and the wild swans that congregated there in the winter, soaring over the lake while the surrounding fells sparkled with snow.

"I used to think I would never see anything more beautiful," he said. There was a smile in his eyes as he looked at her. She looked away, thinking with regret that she had never been paid so lovely or so subtle a compliment.

"Miss Arndale, I must thank you for all you are doing to teach Marianne and Lizzie."

"Your sisters are charming girls. It has been a pleasure teaching them," she replied, relieved at the change of subject. Now if only he would stop looking at her in such a dangerously affectionate manner.

"They are becoming very fond of you, and will miss you very much when it is time for you to end your stay here."

She looked down, troubled by the warmth in his

voice. She knew he was referring to himself as well as his sisters.

"Perhaps I should not visit quite so often, then," she said.

She could have sworn he winced, as if she had struck him. She had not meant to sound so rude, and hastened to make reparation. "I am sorry. I did not mean to be ungrateful. I am very glad of the opportunity to play your instrument, but I do not wish to cause your sisters pain when I leave."

"My sisters would not be the only ones to regret your absence," he said, and now she had no doubt as to his meaning. A foolish joy bubbled up inside her at his words, and she made the mistake of looking back into his eyes. She wrenched her gaze away. She wanted to believe the ardor she saw in his expression, but she knew it was false. His feelings were not real; they would not survive closer acquaintance.

"No! Stop, please! I do not wish to hear this. Let us go back," she said.

She turned and quickly strode back to where the older ladies were sitting. As she did so, she made the mistake of looking at his face. He was frowning, but it was also clear he had not given up hope.

She noticed the Maldons and the Cotterfields had arrived, and were just in the act of descending from their carriages. Miss Maldon was looking even more subdued than usual. Catherine, conscious of the silent Mr. Woodmere at her side, realized she must be the cause of Miss Maldon's dejection.

She had to do something!

She looked around, and saw Captain Maldon standing nearby, surrounded by the Cotterfield girls, who were both giggling and trying to speak to him at once.

He looked up and smiled as Catherine and Mr. Woodmere approached, and she could see that his smile held part amusement and part exasperation. She had noticed at the dinner party that the Miss Cotterfields had all decided to not too subtly set their caps for him. Now an idea occurred to her. Perhaps Captain Maldon needed rescuing?

She returned his smile with a bright one of her own.

"Good morning, Miss Arndale," he said.

"Good morning. A lovely sight, is it not?" she asked, gesturing toward the belt of wild daffodils.

"Not half as lovely as the sight before me," he replied.

The Miss Cotterfields all tittered. Catherine heard a muffled curse from behind her, and knew it came from Mr. Woodmere. She steeled herself to ignore him and continued to smile at Captain Maldon.

"Perhaps you will lend me your arm for another turn amongst the daffodils," she suggested, with another airy smile. Hopefully he would recognize it as an invitation to flirt, and not take it for anything more serious.

It seemed that he understood. Professing himself to be delighted at the prospect, he bowed to the rest of the party and then led Catherine back toward the lakeshore. Catherine saw the others drift on after them in small groups, but keeping their distance.

"Captain Maldon," she said as soon as they were out of earshot. "I hope you will not misunderstand my asking you to come away with me."

"I confess I am grateful to you for rescuing me from the Miss Cotterfields' attentions," he said, with a reassuring twinkle in his eye. "They are perhaps a trifle too, shall we say, enthusiastic, for my company?"

"Perhaps."

"However, I would guess that you had another reason for requesting my escort," he said, looking at her curiously.

She wondered what he had seen.

"Forgive me, but it seemed that when we arrived you were rather upset with Woodmere. He was not forcing any attentions on you, was he?"

"No, of course not."

"But you do not find his admiration welcome? I must admit I do not know him very well, but he seems a capital fellow."

"He is, but before I arrived he was courting Charlotte Maldon, and now I fear it may come to nothing, for he seems to be infatuated with *me* instead."

"Courting my cousin?" he asked, brows furrowed. "Yes, I had heard that but I did not believe it. I thought it just one of my sister-in-law's foolish schemes."

"No, I believe it to be the truth."

"Why ever would he be courting Charlotte?"

"I believe he needs someone to help him care for his family," she replied, feeling more than a little wistful.

"What? That is almost as bad as her wanting to hire herself out as a governess! What is he thinking, to take advantage of her in such a manner?"

Catherine was surprised to see Captain Maldon showing such indignation.

"I believe he is thinking of her best interests, too," she said in a placating tone. "Her lot is not an easy one."

His expression became thoughtful. Catherine saw him turn his head. Following the direction of his gaze, she noticed Mr. Woodmere strolling with Miss Maldon a few hundred yards away. They appeared to be deep in conversation. Perhaps her plan was working. Perhaps Mr. Woodmere was disgusted by her flirtation with Captain Maldon, and was resuming his courtship of Charlotte Maldon.

Catherine told herself she should be happy that matters were returning to their proper course, and satisfied that she had done the right thing. So why did her heart feel as heavy as one of those large stones that lined the lakeshore?

Philip watched Captain Maldon walk off with Miss Arndale in disgust. He would willingly have pitched Maldon into the lake, but he was even more disturbed by Miss Arndale's actions. He could have sworn she was not the sort of female who would toy with men's affections. But then, what *did* he know about her?

They'd known each other for such a brief time, yet he had felt an instant, powerful attraction to her, a sense that he had finally, against all expectation, found the soul mate he had thought did not exist. Was it impossible to think that she might feel the same way? He was nearly sure he'd caught a glimpse of joy in her expression when he'd tried to profess his feelings to her. He'd had the distinct impression that she both desired and dreaded his advances, and that that was why she had encouraged Maldon. He would not be able to rest until he found out.

However, there was nothing he could do at present. Looking about him, he noticed Charlotte still standing by the Maldons' carriage. Her expression was more desolate than he'd ever seen.

He hastened to her side.

"Are you unwell, Charlotte?" he asked.

"No," she said, shaking her head. "I am only tired. Mama and I have only just moved into the cottage, and I have been very busy trying to make her comfortable."

"Perhaps a stroll will do you good," he suggested, offering his arm.

She agreed, but without any sign of enthusiasm.

As they walked, Philip watched Charlotte's face. The look of strain he saw there seemed more than what might be caused by mere housekeeping worries.

"I wish I could help you in some way," he said. "I hate to see you so unhappy."

"You have already offered what you could," she replied, sighing. "But it would be wrong for us to marry when *both* are longing for others."

She looked ahead, toward Miss Arndale and Captain Maldon, and then back at Philip. "You need not dissemble, Philip. You have formed a strong partiality for Miss Arndale, have you not?"

He nodded, although he could have found better words to describe his feelings.

"I can only counsel you to beware," she said. "I do not trust her."

Philip started at her accusing tone. He'd never heard Charlotte speak with such venom.

"She saved Lizzie's life."

"That is true. Forgive me, I had not meant to be malicious. But you must admit there is some mystery about her. I fear she may wound you somehow."

He looked down, unable to answer. Charlotte's words only echoed his own fears, and yet somehow his heart persisted in believing in Miss Arndale.

* * *

A half hour later, Catherine and Captain Maldon returned to the carriages along with the others to partake of the food and wine that had been brought along. Catherine was dismayed to see that neither Mr. Woodmere nor Miss Maldon looked happier than when she had left them. His expression was grave, and hers even more subdued than before, if that was possible.

After the meal, one of the Cotterfield girls proposed a walk up Gowbarrow Fell, where a relatively short climb would take them to a pleasant vantage point overlooking the lake. Catherine was not surprised that most of the younger members of the group thought it a delightful idea, but she decided she would have to forego the pleasure this time. Miss Maldon had declared herself too tired to climb the fell, and Catherine knew she could not give up the opportunity to talk to her and learn what was amiss.

Soon, the rest of the party headed off for their walk, leaving Catherine and Miss Maldon with the older ladies of the party. Catherine was surprised to see Aunt Phoebe look longingly after the departing group and murmur something to Aunt Mattie, who answered more audibly, telling her sister not to be a fool. It almost seemed as if Aunt Phoebe had wished to go along. The poor dear! This wasn't the first time Catherine had seen Aunt Phoebe chafe at the limitations of her health. Sometimes Catherine feared her frail aunt would rebel, and do something to dangerously overtax her weak heart.

However, Aunt Mattie had Aunt Phoebe well in hand at present, so Catherine was able to turn her attention back to Miss Maldon, who had gone toward the lake and was standing moodily looking out over the water. Catherine approached her and gently asked her if she was well.

"I am perfectly well," retorted Miss Maldon. "I do not need or desire your solicitude, Miss Arndale."

Catherine winced at Miss Maldon's bitter retort. However, she could not blame her for feeling hurt and defensive.

"I am so sorry, Miss Maldon. Please trust me when I say I never meant to attach Mr. Woodmere," she said. "Truly, it is just an infatuation on his part, and I *assure* you I will do everything I can to discourage it."

Miss Maldon turned and stared at Catherine for a moment. "Do you believe I envy you for having attracted Philip's interest?" she asked.

Catherine felt confused, but she nodded. "That is why I went off with Captain Maldon. Was I wrong?"

Miss Maldon gave a brittle laugh, and it was Catherine's turn to stare.

"I refused Philip's offer weeks ago."

"You did? But my aunts gave me to understand—"

"They were wrong."

"But then—why are you so angry with me? Oh dear, it isn't Captain Maldon, is it?"

"It is none of your business!" said Miss Maldon in a snappish tone.

"But it is. I would never have tried to flirt with him if I had known. I have hurt you, but I promise I only meant well," she said. "Why do I always make such a botch of things?"

Miss Maldon sighed, and the anger seemed to go out of her. "I believe you did mean well," she said. "I must apologize. I should not have behaved so rudely. It doesn't really matter."

Miss Maldon's listless manner bothered Catherine even more than her earlier irritability.

"Does Captain Maldon know of your feelings for him?" she asked.

"No one knows," Miss Maldon replied. "Please do not say anything. I would die of mortification!"

Miss Maldon sniffed. Catherine decided it might do her good to have a little cry, and to tell her troubles to a sympathetic confidante.

"Come, let us sit down," she said, gesturing toward a smooth boulder near the water's side. She sat down, and Miss Maldon obediently followed, with a quick glance behind her as if to see if the other ladies had seen her distress. Miss Maldon let a few sobs out, and Catherine lent her a handkerchief. After Miss Maldon had blown her nose, she seemed more composed.

"Perhaps you would like to talk about it?" asked Catherine. "I promise not to tell anyone what you say. When did you first meet Captain Maldon?"

"He came to visit several years ago, for a summer. Although he was very friendly to me, he was always flirting with Mary and Louisa. I am sure he never noticed me; I never could match their liveliness. Now it is happening all over again."

Catherine remembered how very indignant Captain Maldon had been over Mr. Woodmere's plan to marry Miss Maldon. It occurred to her that the case might not be as hopeless as Miss Maldon seemed to think.

"Well, Miss Maldon, I do not think he appreciates their *liveliness* quite as much as you think. I suspect he would find your more rational conversation a relief from their silliness."

Miss Maldon looked doubtful. "Do you think so? Do you think I should let him know my feelings?"

"That is what *I* would do," said Catherine instantly.

"I should not dare be so bold! And it is hopeless, anyway."

Miss Maldon's shocked expression made Catherine reconsider. She remembered Captain Maldon's reaction to the Cotterfield girls' pursuit, and decided perhaps Miss Maldon's instincts were not completely at fault.

"Perhaps you are right," she said. "But I must tell you something. Captain Maldon knows the Cotterfield girls are setting their caps at him. At present he is feeling rather *hunted.* I think he might find some comfort in resuming your earlier friendship. If you care for him, it is the least you can do to rescue him from the Miss Cotterfields' attentions."

"Perhaps I could do that," said Miss Maldon.

Catherine saw a thoughtful expression appear on her companion's face, and congratulated herself on her strategy.

"Would it do any harm if you tried smiling at him occasionally?" she added. "And surely it is time for you to put off your mourning and wear something a trifle more cheerful?"

"I could not. Mama and I have not the means—"

"Do not worry about that! I have plenty of dresses, more than I will ever need while I am here. I am sure we could shorten some of them for you."

"Oh, I could not accept your dresses," said Miss Maldon, looking tempted.

"I insist. It is the least I can do, after the wretched mull I've made of things."

It took only a little more encouragement for Miss Maldon to accept the offer. Catherine continued to chat with her, her spirits rising at the prospect of helping Miss Maldon win Captain Maldon's affections.

Only when they spied the other members of the party, returning from their climb up Gowbarrow Fell, did Catherine wonder at the source of her happiness. Was she really just glad to help Miss Maldon, or was she secretly relieved to learn that Mr. Woodmere was unattached?

That was a mistake indeed.

As the crowd drew closer, Catherine could easily make out Mr. Woodmere among the group, Lizzie riding on his shoulders. Catherine could not help smiling at the sight. The Corsair, with a dainty fairy on his shoulders!

Then Catherine saw him looking at her. He had clearly noticed her impulsive smile. He raised his eyebrows slightly, then a hopeful light appeared in his eyes. He looked as if he wished to speak to her. However, there was no opportunity for private conversation as the party reunited and those who had climbed the fell busied themselves with exclaiming at the excellence of the views, and condoling with those who could not see them.

A few minutes later, they all set off to see the park's other attractions. A short walk through the trees brought them to Lyulph's Tower, a hunting lodge styled to resemble a castle, which the Duke of Norfolk, who owned the park, had built there.

At close quarters Catherine thought it looked a trifle too modern, but Mr. Woodmere assured her that when viewed across the lake, the effect was as romantic as one could wish. He spoke as if he hoped to show it to her one day, and it was all she could do not to reveal how tempting she found the prospect.

He continued to walk by her side as they walked about a quarter of a mile to see the nearby waterfall. The main cataract descended perhaps eighty feet, thundering down a wooded ravine full of ferns and other moisture- and shade-loving plants.

It was a lovely, undeniably romantic sight, and Catherine stood rapt in enjoyment of it, for a moment forgetting her other concerns. Then she noticed that their group had begun to disperse a little, some climbing up further into the glen to view the upper cascades, and others finding places to sit on nearby rocks. She watched Mr. Woodmere follow his brothers and sisters up the path, and found herself a seat in a secluded spot near the main cataract.

A few minutes later, she jumped, startled by the sight of Mr. Woodmere coming to sit beside her. She had not heard his approach over the rushing sound of the waterfall.

"I'm sorry, Miss Arndale. I did not mean to startle you," he said, bending close to her so as to be heard.

She could feel his breath on her cheek. It felt warm in contrast to the cool misty air of the ravine. Warm, and unexpectedly seductive.

She started to rise, but he gently put a hand on hers to detain her.

"Please do not run away. I must speak to you," he said.

She sat back down, not knowing quite why. He quickly withdrew his hand. She looked around. The other members of the party were close by, some of them just yards away. However, they did not seem to have noticed anything, nor would they be able to overhear them over the roar of the falls.

It felt disturbingly private.

"I'm sorry I distressed you earlier," he said. "I only hoped to tell you what was in my heart. I—"

"Don't say it! What you are feeling is just gratitude, just an infatuation."

"Is that what you think? Is that why you went off with Maldon?"

A tremor of guilt shook her again at how she had hurt him by affecting to flirt with Captain Maldon. It would be prudent to maintain the pretense. However, she found she could not be prudent, not when he was sitting so close by, and watching her with such a keen, anxious expression.

All she wanted to do was to explain herself, so he would not think ill of her.

"I thought you and Miss Maldon were on the verge of becoming betrothed before I came," she said. "I did not wish to spoil things for you and your family."

"I thought perhaps that was it," he said eagerly. He leaned back slightly, breathing a sigh of relief. Her own heart felt irrationally lighter at his words, and she had to remind herself again that she was a far worse match for Mr. Woodmere than Charlotte would have been.

"I'll admit I did plan to marry Charlotte," he continued. "For all the best practical reasons. I will forever be grateful to her for refusing me. Now that I have met you—"

"Do not say it," she interrupted. "We have been acquainted for such a short time. You cannot love me. You don't know me!"

"I know you are brave and true, and would do anything for those you care for. I can see it in your eyes, hear it in your voice. It's all I need to know."

She felt sudden tears forming in the corners of her eyes, and looked away from him.

"Forgive me. I see I've spoken too soon," he said.

She could swear she felt his breath on the back of her neck, warm, caressing, inexorably tempting her to turn around and face him again.

"It will never be the right time," she said, distressed at the troubled look she saw in his eyes. "There are circumstances. I cannot explain, but it is impossible."

"Yes, I know you harbor some dark secret," he said, a rueful half smile on his face. "Whatever it is, I can't believe it is as bad as you think. I wish you would trust me. I am not easily shocked."

She stifled a wild impulse to take him at his word. He did not know what he was asking. He would be horrified if he knew she had nearly eloped with an infamous rake. Perhaps the truth would be the kindest way to end matters, but she found she could not bear the thought of him looking away from her in disgust.

Besides, she had promised her aunts she would not tell.

She shook her head.

"At least tell me this," he said. "You are not already . . . entangled, or in love with another man, are you?"

"No, I am not."

He drew in a deep breath; she could see how relieved he was. "And is there a chance—even the slightest chance—that you might come to return my feelings?"

Her heart beat urgently at the raw emotion in his voice. This was the time to lie to him, to forever dissuade him from pursuing her. She had only to look him in the eye and say no. But she could not.

Weak fool! She could not do it.

After a moment of her silence, he smiled. There was a dangerous light in his eyes, a determined set to his chin.

"Very well, Miss Arndale," he said. "I can be patient. One day soon you *will* confide in me."

Eight

Penelope looked about Hyde Park with distaste. Even at an uncrowded, unfashionable early morning hour, she could not help associating the place with the tedious and mortifying ritual she endured there almost every fine afternoon. She hated having to sit beside her aunt in her uncle's barouche, for which they were still being dunned, and cringe as her aunt did her best to attract the attention of affluent suitors for her hand.

With relief, she saw Juliana alighting from her carriage near their appointed meeting spot, and ran forward to greet her. They embraced, and began to walk on a path that paralleled the Serpentine, their maids following at a discreet distance.

"Why are we meeting *here?*" she asked. "Is it something to do with Catherine?"

Juliana nodded. "I hope that this morning we shall discover the truth."

"But why Hyde Park? What have you found out? Is there any good news?"

Juliana paused, looking as if she wanted to choose her words carefully. Penelope's heart sank. The news must not be good.

"I'm not sure, dear," said Juliana. "I have been having Thomas—one of our footmen, you know—make some discreet inquiries. He is very good at such things, and always appreciates a little extra money to send home to his mother. He has learned that Verwood did leave London the day after the Hethertons' ball. But he has returned now. Alone, I'm afraid."

"Dear God!" said Penelope. "He must have deserted Catherine! I wonder if there is some way we can discover where she is, and help her somehow?"

"That is what I hope to learn today. Mind, Pen, we don't know for certain that Verwood made off with her."

"Why else would he have left London, if not to elope with Cat? Why would he return to town without her, if they are married?"

"I don't know. That is what we are here to find out."

"We are?"

"Yes. Thomas has it on good authority that Lord Verwood exercises his horse here in the Park every morning. We are going to confront him."

Juliana's eyes were bright with determination, but Pen's stomach fluttered nervously at the prospect. She always dreaded confrontations, but this one promised to be even worse than their abortive call at Whitgrave House. What chance did she and Jule have against a notorious scoundrel like Verwood?

Very little, she feared, but they would have to try, nonetheless.

"Do you know what he looks like?" she asked Juliana.

"Thomas says he is a little taller than the average, and dark. He usually rides a dark bay with a star on his forehead."

"Do you think *they* will let us talk to him?" she asked, looking back at their maids.

"They will keep us in sight, but no more. I have told Polly I am here to meet a lord," said Juliana, looking a bit mischievous. "She knows Grandpapa wishes me to marry one, so she will allow it, and keep your maid from interfering as well. Of course, I have not told her Verwood is a mere baron!"

Pen gave Juliana a sympathetic smile. A few impoverished lords of the requisite rank had already asked permission to woo her friend, but Juliana had spurned them all. Of course, no gentleman had expressed the slightest interest in *her* yet.

They strolled on in silence for a few more minutes, both watching the few horsemen who were about so early, looking for a horse and rider that answered Thomas's description.

"I see him!" said Juliana excitedly.

"Where?" asked Penelope.

"There! Riding along the Serpentine!"

Penelope followed the direction of Juliana's finger. There in the distance, she saw him: a tall gentleman in a black coat, riding a bay horse with a star on his forehead. They were cantering along the water, coming in their direction. The lovely thoroughbred and his obviously skilled rider made quite a picture. For an instant, Pen wished she had paper and pencil with her to sketch the image.

Out of the corner of her eye, she saw Juliana raise her hand and wave to the oncoming rider, but he gave no sign of seeing them. In fact, he increased his pace, urging his mount to extend his pace to a gallop.

"He is ignoring us!" cried Pen.

"We can't let him." Juliana turned and began to swiftly run across the narrow stretch of grass that separated the path from the bridleway. Penelope picked up her skirts and followed suit, leaning forward and pumping her shorter legs as fast as she could in order to keep up with Juliana's longer stride.

"Pen! Stop!" Juliana screamed, and Pen realized she'd overtaken her friend and was almost onto the bridleway. She tried to stop herself, but her foot caught in her skirts and she tumbled headlong, right into the oncoming horseman's path. For a nightmarishly slow moment, she struggled to get up, feeling half paralyzed by fear. She was going to be trampled!

Miraculously, Verwood's horse plunged to a halt.

An instant later, Juliana was kneeling by Pen's side.

"Are you hurt?" she asked.

Pen sat up and shook her head, conscious that Verwood was looking down at both of them with a thunderous expression. Eyes so dark they were almost black bored into her as he vented his frustration.

"What possessed you to get in my way?" he shouted, as his horse sidled and tossed his head. "I could have killed you! I hope my horse hasn't overreached himself."

He dismounted and began to examine his horse's forelegs. Meanwhile, Juliana helped Penelope up and motioned to their frightened maids to keep their distance.

Now that it was all over, Pen shuddered at the thought of her narrow escape, and at the fury she heard in Verwood's voice. Scoundrel though he was, he had some right to be angry. She hoped his poor horse wasn't injured.

"Is—is he hurt?" Pen asked, annoyed to hear her voice sound so shaken. She had to pull herself together, so she and Juliana could question Verwood.

"No thanks to either of you," he said in a curt tone,

but Pen could see he looked relieved. "How could you do something so idiotic?"

"We are sorry. We needed to speak to you, but we could not get your attention," said Juliana.

Pen saw him relax a little more, then look her and Juliana over slowly and thoroughly. She felt herself flushing with annoyance. Of course, a rake would do just such an assessment of any unfortunate females he met.

"Ah, but I must beg *your* forgiveness," he said, sweeping them a graceful bow. "It was unpardonably rude of me to scold you so. Please believe that my words were prompted by concern for the safety of two such enchanting young ladies."

He smiled at them appreciatively, then patted his horse and added, "And I must admit, this *is* my favorite hack."

Pen suppressed an unexpected urge to smile back. She reminded herself that such roguish charm was only to be expected of a successful rake, and that his apology most likely sprang from admiration for Juliana's golden good looks.

"Never mind about your horse," said Juliana. "We are here to discover what you have done with Lady Catherine."

Verwood's lazy smile vanished.

"I take it you are the friends Lady Catherine spoke of, Miss Hutton and Miss, er, Talcott?" They nodded. "And you wish to know what *I* have done with her?"

"Yes," said Juliana. "We know Cat planned to elope with you, and we want to know where she is."

He stared thoughtfully at them both for a moment.

"I cannot tell you," he replied.

Pen felt a sudden, unaccustomed rage take hold of her at his bland tone.

"Oh, you miserable rogue! You've abandoned her somewhere, haven't you?" she cried. She ran forward, ready to claw at his handsome face.

"Calm yourself, little hornet," he said, grasping her hands and holding her at arm's length.

"Let her go!" said Juliana.

Verwood continued to hold Penelope's hands.

"In a moment," he said, in a soft, carefully indifferent voice. "I see my reputation has preceded me, but despite what you may think, I have not seduced, nor have I abandoned your friend Lady Catherine. There is no need to rip my eyes out on her account."

"Why should we believe you?" Pen asked, determined not to succumb to his soothing voice.

He sighed. "Because I can prove it."

Though still unconvinced, she relaxed, and he released her hands. She felt the blood rush back into them, and realized just how hard he had gripped them. Shakily, she stepped backward to stand by Juliana again, hoping Verwood would not see how she trembled. She still didn't know what had possessed her to attack him so boldly.

"If you will walk with me, I will tell you all I know," he said.

They fell in beside him as he began to walk his horse along the ride. He reached into an inner pocket of his riding coat and pulled out a folded paper.

"Here," he said, handing it to Juliana. "I received this the day of the Hethertons' ball."

He led his horse slowly onward, while Juliana and Penelope stopped for a minute to read the brief note.

"This is not Catherine's hand," said Juliana, when they had caught back up to him.

"No, it is not," Pen concurred. "She did not change her mind about eloping with you. We saw her ourselves at the Hethertons' ball, just before she was to meet with you."

"I suspected as much," he said. "When I first read the note, I was angry, but the next day when I had had some time to reflect on it, I thought it seemed out of character. I went to Whitgrave House, hoping to discover the truth, but I was refused admittance and told that Lady Catherine had gone into the country for her health. I assumed that she had been taken to Whitgrave Castle, so I drove there as quickly as I could, only to find that she was not there. Since then I have been trying to decide whether the letter was a forgery or not, and wondering if I should continue searching, or if Lady Catherine is safe somewhere, laughing at me."

His expression was completely sober now, even grim, and Pen realized he was telling the truth.

"Do you love her?" she asked.

He looked at her and Juliana, then shrugged. "I want her for my wife. Now that you both assure me she did not have a change of heart, I shall try again to find her. Does either of you have any idea where the duke might have sent her?"

Juliana shook her head. "Pen, what do you think?"

"I am afraid—no, I don't want to say it!"

"What?" asked Verwood.

"I know this sounds perfectly Gothic," she said nervously. "But I fear he has her locked away somewhere, perhaps in an asylum for the insane. He has enough money and the influence to do such a thing, and he has always seemed such an unnatural father."

Pen looked at Juliana and at Verwood, hoping they would laugh at her lurid imaginings, and felt a chill creep through her when they did not.

Then Verwood spoke, in a reassuring tone. "I think it is most likely that he has packed her off to some obscure relations. I shall make some inquiries."

Pen was not sure he was not merely trying to comfort her and Juliana, but she felt a little relieved nonetheless. She also felt her conscience prick her. It seemed she owed Verwood an apology.

"I am sorry for saying what I did about you," she said.

"Your conclusion was quite understandable under the circumstances," he said coolly. "Don't make a hero of me, Miss Talcott. I assure you, I have my own perfectly selfish reasons for wishing to marry your friend."

Verwood's words and their delivery seemed completely dispassionate, yet Pen sensed some mystery behind them. Perhaps he loved Catherine, but did not wish to admit it? It certainly did seem as if he wanted to appear as heartless as he had been painted. Then again, he might have some nefarious purpose in mind for Catherine.

"Do not look so distressed," he said, addressing himself to her and Juliana. "I have no intention of harming Lady Catherine. Quite the reverse, I assure you."

"You had better not be lying!" she said.

"I am not," he said, smiling more naturally now. "Lady Catherine is fortunate in possessing such devoted friends."

"Will you promise not to give up until you find her?" asked Juliana.

"I promise. In turn, you must promise to inform me if either of you hears from her. Here is my direction," he said, handing his card to Penelope. "You must not fret, either of you. I fear this may be a rather long and tedious search."

"We wish you luck," said Juliana. Pen nodded.

In a swift, graceful movement, Verwood remounted his horse.

"Au revoir!" he said, tipped his hat to them, and rode off.

Juliana and Pen exchanged glances.

"Do you think he'll find her?" Juliana asked.

Penelope watched Verwood as he cantered off, looking relaxed and elegant and perfectly one with his mount. His demeanor certainly inspired confidence, and she suspected he had means and sources of information she and Jule could not hope to match. But could they trust him?

"I don't know," she said. "I hope so. And I do hope Cat is well, wherever she is."

Nine

Following the excursion to Gowbarrow Park, Catherine conscientiously tried to limit her visits to Woodmere Hall. However, Lizzie and Marianne both pleaded with her with such looks of puzzlement and hurt in their soulful eyes that she found herself promising to resume their daily lessons.

Truth be told, she was not as reluctant as she should have been. She enjoyed Marianne and Lizzie's company as much as she enjoyed their pianoforte. If she also found pleasure in occasionally being escorted home to Larkspur Cottage by their eldest brother, well, she could not help that either.

She tried to tell herself she was merely infatuated, that it was just Mr. Woodmere's deep voice and manly physique that drew her, but that became increasingly difficult as he talked with her of music and poetry, of books they had both read. She had never before met a gentleman who appeared so sincerely to share her every interest, and one, moreover, who felt like a kindred spirit to whom she could confide anything.

It was a constant struggle to conceal the improper nature of her musical tastes and the even more improper nature of her attraction to him. However, she was determined not to do anything that would ruin what was rapidly becoming one of the most halcyon periods in her life.

For she now enjoyed far greater freedom than she ever had. As April gave way to May, Aunt Mattie persuaded Ned and Jemima, as they all called them now, that it was no longer necessary to dog every one of Catherine's footsteps. Ned was on his way to becoming a capital gardener; Catherine found daily amusement in watching him work under Aunt Phoebe's direction, rather like a huge mastiff being commanded by a kitten. Jemima was busy learning the fine points of needlework from Aunt Mattie, and applying her newfound knowledge to the alteration of some of Catherine's dresses for Charlotte Maldon.

Catherine's erstwhile guards no longer complained about the silence of the valley. Indeed, she could have sworn that even in the month they had been there the fresh air and wholesome country fare had done the two Londoners immeasurable good. Their faces seemed cleaner, less sharp-featured, and somehow younger. Even their voices sounded just a trifle softer, though she suspected there would always be a trace of Cockney in their speech.

Catherine sometimes thought they were all undergoing some sort of mystical transformation in this hidden, out-of-the-way place. It was dangerously pleasant to imagine that she was in truth Miss Catherine Arndale of Larkspur Cottage, with no scandals in her past, and that that same Miss Catherine Arndale might be a suitable match for Woodmere of Woodmere Hall. . . .

"Try it again, Marianne."

Catherine watched Marianne grimace, and stumble

back through the tricky passage of the Haydn sonata she'd been attempting to learn.

"Again, but try it a little more slowly, dear," she said, realizing with amusement how much she sounded like a governess. Most of the teachers at Miss Stratton's school would undoubtedly be shocked to see her now!

"Oh, I'll never learn to play half so well as you do!" Marianne slammed her fist down on the keyboard.

Catherine winced at the discord. She wondered what had occurred to put Marianne out of temper; Marianne had never been so fractious during her lessons before.

"I suppose we have played enough today," she said. "What is it? I can see something is troubling you."

"It is Philip. He refuses to see that I am a grown woman now," said Marianne glumly.

Catherine forced herself to suppress the smile that rose to her lips. Although only three years Marianne's senior, she suddenly felt centuries older. But she knew it would annoy Marianne no end to be patronized.

"What did your brother do?" she asked in a friendly tone that invited confidence.

"He chided me for encouraging Charles Cotterfield's attentions. He doesn't understand that I am in love!"

"Did he forbid you to speak to Charles?"

"No, but Charles came to ask permission to pay his addresses, and Philip told him I was too young, and we would have to wait!"

"I can see how annoying that would be. Are you certain you wish to get married so soon?"

"Yes! One never knows what might happen. One of us might die, and leave the other to regret forever what might have been!"

Catherine stifled the laugh that arose in her throat at Marianne's dramatics. She also felt a surge of pity, sensing that Marianne's impatience stemmed from her parents' sudden death. Perhaps it did seem to Marianne that there was no time to wait for love. Still, Catherine found herself in complete accord with Mr. Woodmere's decision. He might not have gone about the matter in the most diplomatic manner, though.

"Perhaps your brother worries that you would regret an early marriage in the same way," she suggested.

"He says so, but he's wrong. If he loved me, he would not take away my best chance for happiness!"

Marianne's defiant tone reminded Catherine of her own feelings when thwarted by her father and stepmother. But there was a world of difference here.

"Your brother does love you, Marianne. You know that, don't you?"

Marianne nodded reluctantly. "But what shall I do? I can't bear to submit tamely to his decrees."

"I can understand how difficult that would be," said Catherine.

"Could you speak to Philip on our behalf? Perhaps you could persuade him to give his consent. Please."

Catherine was not proof against Marianne's pleading, nor the expression in her lustrous brown eyes. She had discovered that it was difficult to refuse any of the Woodmeres when they looked at her in just that way.

Not impossible, though.

"I am sorry," she said, shaking her head. "I have to admit I agree with your brother. Don't you think—"

"No, not you, too!"

"Marianne, listen to me. Your brother—"

"I don't need to listen to this! I thought you were

my friend!" Marianne jumped up, her face stormy, and left the room.

Catherine watched her leave, stunned and hurt by the sudden change in their relations. She had only tried to help, in the best way she knew how. Now she had alienated Marianne. Oh, why had she thought she could advise her? What did she know about raising young ladies? Or about normal family life, for that matter?

Nothing in her background had prepared her for this. In the aristocratic circle in which she had been raised, one made dynastic marriages. After providing one's highborn husband with an heir, one could have discreet affairs. It was by no means expected that one would raise one's own children, or create a loving family circle such as the one enjoyed by the Woodmeres.

She should have known she would make a botch of it. Much as she enjoyed teaching Lizzie and Marianne, and giving Charlotte Maldon a new touch, she was an impostor here, and always would be.

She got up from the chair where she had been sitting and went to the pianoforte. She sat down, and idly began to play the Haydn sonata Marianne had left propped open atop the instrument. However, its graceful cadences were out of tune with her current mood. After several futile attempts to start other pieces, she got up and restlessly went to look out the window.

The sky had been overcast all morning, but now the wind had risen, and darker clouds were rolling in over the western fells. She knew she should leave, but felt a strange reluctance to do so. She went back to the pianoforte and sat down, idly caressing the keys with her hands while struggling against the temptation to play her beloved Beethoven.

What did it matter? This was probably the last time she would teach Marianne anyway. Perhaps no one would hear. On the other hand, what if someone did? She decided to compromise. She could play just one little movement. The introduction to the sonata in E flat should be safe enough.

Philip caught sight of Marianne running up the stairs as he entered the house. Blast! She still looked upset. He paused in the hall, trying to decide what to do next. It was probably useless to speak with Marianne when she was in such a temper. It was such a shame. She'd been so much more cheerful of late, spending a trifle less time reading and a little more time out of doors, smiling more than brooding. He'd set much of it down to Miss Arndale's good influence.

Sadly, it seemed that Marianne had now quarreled with *her* as well. Anxiety gnawed at him as he wondered what his sister might do next. Perhaps he could talk to Miss Arndale about her. Although still disturbingly evasive on most other subjects, she had become fond of his sisters and was always willing to discuss their progress with him.

However, he decided regretfully that she must be already gone. The pianoforte was silent. Perhaps Marianne had driven her away with her tantrums, or perhaps she had left early to avoid the storm that had been threatening all day. Indeed, the whole house was unusually silent. He supposed Dorothea was still giving Lizzie her lessons up in the nursery. The boys must not have returned from their own daily lessons at the

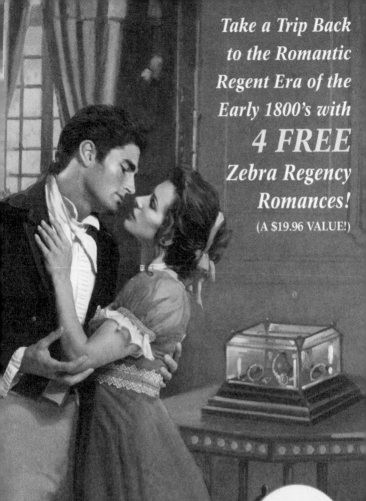

We'd Like to Invite You to Subscribe to Zebra's Regency Romance Book Club and Give You a Gift of 4 Free Books as Your Introduction! (Worth $19.96!)

If you're a Regency lover, imagine the joy of getting 4 FREE Zebra Regency Romances and then the chance to have these lovely stories delivered to your home each month at the lowest price available! Well, that's our offer to you and here's how you benefit by becoming a Regency Romance subscriber:

- 4 FREE Introductory Regency Romances are delivered to your doorstep

- 4 BRAND NEW Regencies are then delivered each month (usually before they're available in bookstores)

- Subscribers save almost $4.00 every month

- Home delivery is always FREE

- You also receive a FREE monthly newsletter, which features author profiles, discounts, subscriber benefits, book previews and more

- No risks or obligations...in other words, you can cancel whenever you wish with no questions asked

Join the thousands of readers who enjoy the savings and convenience offered to Regency Romance subscribers. After your initial introductory shipment, you receive 4 brand-new Zebra Regency Romances each month to examine for 10 days. Then, if you decide to keep the books, you'll pay the preferred subscriber's price of just $4.00 per title. That's only $16.00 for all 4 books and there's never an extra charge for shipping and handling.

It's a no-lose proposition, so return the FREE BOOK CERTIFICATE today!

Say Yes to 4 Free Books!

Complete and return the order card to receive this $19.96 value, ABSOLUTELY FREE!

If the certificate is missing below, write to:
Regency Romance Book Club
P.O. Box 5214, Clifton, New Jersey 07015-5214
or call TOLL-FREE 1-888-345-BOOK

Visit our website at www.kensingtonbooks.com.

FREE BOOK CERTIFICATE

YES! Please rush me 4 Zebra Regency Romances without cost or obligation. I understand that each month thereafter I will be able to preview 4 brand-new Regency Romances FREE for 10 days. Then, if I should decide to keep them, I will pay the money-saving preferred subscriber's price of just $16.00 for all 4...that's a savings of almost $4 off the publisher's price with no additional charge for shipping and handling. I may return any shipment within 10 days and owe nothing, and I may cancel this subscription at any time. My 4 FREE books will be mine to keep in any case.

Name _____

Address _____ Apt. _____

City _____ State _____ Zip _____

Telephone ( ) _____

Signature _____ RN091A
(If under 18, parent or guardian must sign.)

Terms and prices subject to change. Orders subject to acceptance by Regency Romance Book Club.
Offer valid in U.S. only.

vicarage, although if they didn't come home soon they risked being soaked to the skin. Feeling restless, Philip went toward his study.

He was on the threshold when he heard music coming from the drawing room. It sounded like a simple enough tune, then he gradually became aware of deeper undercurrents. Gently it murmured to him, comforting, soothing, and yet somehow wistful. He stepped softly into the hall, the better to hear, and stood listening as the sweet melody gave way to a livelier, more forceful one, only to return and gently fade away.

There was a pause. He took a few steps toward the drawing room, but stopped as he heard Miss Arndale begin to play again. This time it was a darker music, rippling and cascading, the end of each phrase accented with forceful staccato notes. Full of passion. He'd never heard anything like it before.

He peered through the threshold of the drawing room as she began another movement, slow and reflective, with an understated pathos. She looked so very lovely, her eyes half closed, her slim body swaying ever so subtly in time with the music. He didn't dare interrupt. He didn't even want to breathe as he watched her silently from the shadows beyond the doorway.

The slow melody ended, and she launched into an exuberantly lively tune which sounded like the finale. Philip listened in wonder as she transitioned from a bold, intricate passage to a contrasting theme as tender as a love song. He saw the flush of concentration on her face as she returned to the earlier bold theme, her look of exultation as she drove out the final notes, rising, mounting to a glorious final chord.

She sat back and sighed, looking more relaxed than he'd ever seen her. Then she looked up, and saw him there. With infinite regret, he saw her straighten and look up at him with mingled shock and defiance.

"How long have you been there?" she asked, in a tight voice.

"A while," he replied. "I am sorry. I would have made you aware of my presence, but I did not wish to interrupt."

She got up, folding her arms in front of her, looking even more guarded than usual. He *had* to know why.

"What was that you were playing?" he asked.

"The Sonata in E flat, by Ludwig van Beethoven."

"I've never heard anything like it. It was marvelous. Why have you not played it before?"

She looked skeptical. In the same controlled voice, she replied, "Many consider Beethoven's music inappropriate for ladies to play."

"They are fools."

She lowered her hands back to her sides, and it seemed she relaxed just a little.

He smiled. "So is this your dark secret, Miss Arndale? That you've a fondness for such music?"

Looking away, she replied, "It is but one of my besetting vices."

Her tone was light, but he could clearly hear the bitterness behind it. He wondered what, or who, had made her feel she had to hide this amazing gift of hers.

"If making such music is a vice, may you never reform."

She looked back at him then, and he saw surprise and a hint of yearning in her expression.

Swiftly, he crossed the room and took her hands in his, rejoicing when she did not protest. He looked down at them and marveled at their elegant suppleness.

"So strong. So very beautiful," he murmured.

Impulsively, he lifted her hands to his lips. He gently kissed them, exploring the delicate, slender contours of her fingers, savoring the peachlike softness of her skin.

He heard her let out a slight gasp. He looked up, and saw his own desire mirrored in her blue eyes, dark as midnight. He released her hands, slowly gathered her into his arms, and pulled her close. She tensed slightly, and he prayed she was not about to retreat behind her prim facade again.

"Please trust me," he said.

"I do trust you," she said, leaning her forehead into his chest. "But I do not trust myself."

He bent his head down and kissed the top of her head, all he could reach. Her silky hair brushed his lips as she raised her head back up to look at him, and he felt as if he might burst with longing for her. Why did she look so torn?

"Trust *this,*" he whispered, and kissed her lips briefly.

She stood perfectly still, but he could hear and feel her quickening breath. She tilted her face up toward him, lips slightly parted. He pulled her closer, thrilling when she raised her arms up around him to return his embrace. He kissed her again, this time deepening the kiss, taking time to taste and savor the joy of it.

Then she gave out a soft moan. Quite suddenly, she stiffened again and pulled away. His whole being ached with disappointment at the loss. Why had she withdrawn from him?

Catherine turned away from Mr. Woodmere. Her

limbs felt oddly shaky, but somehow she managed to take a few steps away from him, toward the window.

Fool! Wanton fool! She'd ruined everything now. She couldn't bear to face him. He must despise her.

"What is wrong?" he asked softly.

The gentleness of his voice drew her to turn around. To her total surprise, he did not look the slightest bit shocked. Instead, he stood gazing at her with affectionate concern, his hands slightly raised, as if to welcome her back into his arms.

Relief flooded through her, just as it had when he had said he enjoyed her music, and she struggled with a powerful urge to throw herself back into his arms. Then she remembered everything else, and knew she had been cruel to encourage him so.

A sudden gust of wind rattled the windows.

"I must go home," she said, looking out at the ominously darkened skies.

The next instant, they opened up, and a hard rain began to drive against the windows.

"You can't leave now," he said. "It's not fit outside for man nor beast. You'd not be safe even in the carriage."

She knew he was right, that it was folly to go out in such weather, but staying with him seemed even more hazardous.

"Miss Arndale . . . *Catherine,* you must trust me. I'll not kiss you again if you don't wish it. But I'll not let you out during a storm like this either."

She saw the worry in his face, and felt all the irony of it. He clearly feared he had been too forward, that he had offended her maidenly sense of propriety. Didn't he realize she had none?

"I do trust you," she said, determined to be sensible. "I will stay."

He came to stand beside her, and she strove to steady her breath as they both peered out the window. The rain was so heavy she could barely see the other side of the valley.

"Do you think it will end soon?" she asked.

He shook his head.

Catherine remembered Aunt Matilda had tried to dissuade her from coming today. She had said that spring rains like this one often swelled the becks coming down the hillsides, flooding the lanes suddenly and dangerously.

"I'm sorry," said Mr. Woodmere. "I think you may have to spend the night."

"I can't! It's impossible," she protested.

"Your aunts will understand that we couldn't allow you to leave now. Do not fear for your reputation. Remember, my cousin is here. If it would make you more comfortable, I shall call her down. I think Lizzie's lessons should be almost over by now anyway, and Jack and Harry should be home soon, I trust."

It was so kind of him to be concerned for her virtue and her reputation. She couldn't tell him she feared for neither; she was not even sure what it was that she *did* fear.

He looked back toward the windows with a crease between his brows, and she knew he was worrying about his brothers. Then she caught the sound of boisterous laughter and the clomping of boots in the entrance hall.

"Good! They've returned," he said, looking relieved.

"I'm glad," she said. She, too, was relieved the boys

were home. Moreover, with all these chaperones she would not be alone with Mr. Woodmere for much longer.

She found he was watching her, looking troubled.

"Don't be frightened of me, Catherine. Please tell me I haven't spoiled everything by kissing you. For I hope very much you'll let me do it again, sometime soon."

"Mr. Woodmere—" she said.

"Please, call me Philip. At least when we are alone."

"Do you never give up?" she asked.

"No, I am terminally tenacious."

"Philip," she said, and paused. How natural it felt to call him so. "Philip, I don't wish to encourage you in what could only end in pain for both of us."

"I don't need encouragement, love," he said, smiling ruefully. "But I think you enjoyed our kiss at least a little. I can draw some hope from that."

She looked down, wondering if he guessed just how much she'd enjoyed it.

"I see I'll need to be patient a bit longer," he said. "In the meantime, let us sit down. Perhaps you can give me some advice. I've been wishing to talk to you about Marianne."

She resumed her seat at the pianoforte, telling herself she was glad he had changed the subject.

"Yes, she told me the two of you had had a disagreement," she replied. "I tried to counsel her, and ended up provoking her instead. I am sorry. I meant to help, but I am afraid I've only made matters worse."

"Don't berate yourself. Marianne can be quite a handful. I still think you may be able to enter into her feelings more easily than I can. Perhaps you can think of a way to convince her that she should wait until she's met more gentlemen before she settles upon a husband."

"I am honored that you think I might help."

She smiled inwardly at the thought of what the teachers at Miss Stratton's school would say if they knew her advice was being solicited on such a matter.

"Perhaps you have hit upon the answer already," she suggested. "Do you think it might make her feel less trammeled if you were to let her go out into society a bit more? Perhaps start taking her to some of those assemblies at Keswick?"

"Do you think she's old enough? She just turns seventeen next month."

"I think the more you tell her she's not old enough, the more she will fret," she replied. After all, she did know *something* about rebellious young ladies.

"You are probably right. Thank you," he said, with an intimate smile that made the warmth come back to her face.

Then she heard Lizzie's quick footsteps in the hall, and a few seconds later, Lizzie burst into the room.

"Philip! Miss Catherine!" she shouted excitedly, running toward them.

She gave Philip a quick hug, then turned to Catherine.

"Miss Catherine! I am so happy you are still here! Will you have dinner with us?"

"Yes I will," she replied, gathering her little friend into her embrace. "It seems I must stay the night, as well."

"Are you afraid of the storm? *I* am not afraid."

"You are very brave, Lizzie," she replied. Out of the corner of her eye, she caught a hint of anxiety in Philip's face as he looked at his sister.

"Philip keeps me safe when it rains," Lizzie continued. "Philip will keep *you* safe, too."

"How very kind of him," she replied, and saw him grin. She *did* feel safe here, despite the wind and rain buffeting the old stone house. A fire blazed in the hearth, she had a darling little girl in her lap, and Mr. Woodmere—no, *Philip,* watched them both with love in his eyes. She didn't deserve it, and it wouldn't last, but she would savor the moment anyway.

She continued to bask in the same warm feeling throughout dinner. Philip had left her with Lizzie and his cousin, and had gone upstairs. He had talked to Marianne, and brought her down in an apologetic yet cheerful mood. Even the boys' inevitable squabbles didn't disturb her sense of being blissfully far from the ducal family.

Looking around the table, she realized she had never taken part in a family dinner before. At Whitgrave Castle, the children had always taken their meals in the nursery, where her father and stepmother rarely set foot.

After dinner, Philip's cousin took herself off to bed, complaining that storms always gave her the headache and stating her intention to dose herself with some laudanum to ensure a sound night. Catherine followed the rest of the Woodmeres into the drawing room, where they played various games, then listened while Philip read to them from *Guy Mannering.* Catherine had already read the novel, but Philip's rendering of the tale of gypsies and smugglers, complete with the proper Scottish accents, soon had her nearly as engrossed as the children. She wasn't surprised that his brothers and sisters listened with rapt attention, despite the rushing and pattering of rain outside. The storm that had abated somewhat during dinner had now broken out anew, making a return to Larkspur Cottage quite impossible.

Later, the Woodmeres' kind-looking housekeeper escorted Catherine to a comfortable, pretty room adjacent to Lizzie's, telling her it had been Miss Jane's room before she had married and moved to Derbyshire. Marianne came to lend her a nightgown and nightcap, and to apologize for having quarreled with her.

After they had embraced and Marianne had left, Catherine sat up in bed for a while. Normally, she found the sound of rain soothing, but now she felt only restlessness, and she knew the cause.

He was sleeping only two rooms away.

She could not stop thinking about the warmth in Philip's voice as he had praised her music, or the tender way he had kissed her. There was no denying it any longer. Against all her best intentions, she had fallen in love.

She had fallen in love with him, and she had just spent the loveliest evening with his family. It was perilously easy to believe that life could go on like this. She tried to remind herself of all the reasons why this happiness would not last, but lost track of them as she finally drifted toward sleep.

Suddenly, she awoke. The wind had died down earlier, but now it had returned with renewed vigor, once again pelting the house with a new torrent of rain. Mingled with the sounds of the storm she thought she heard crying. She listened for a moment, at first convinced that it was just a strange sound made by the wind. No, it sounded like Lizzie.

She hesitated for another moment, wondering if

someone would go to the child. When no one did, she got out of bed. Marianne had had no dressing gown to lend her, so she wrapped the shawl she had worn earlier around her shoulders. She lit her candle and went into the hall.

She could still hear Lizzie sobbing. The rest of the house was quiet; apparently no one else could hear. She opened Lizzie's door, and entered. Lizzie was still lying down, curled up into a little ball at one end of her small bed. As Catherine came closer, she could see that Lizzie's eyes were still closed. She was crying in her sleep.

Catherine wondered if it was wrong to wake her, but she couldn't leave her sounding so miserable. She set down her candle, sat down on the bed beside Lizzie and began to stroke her back gently, hoping to comfort her back to a more peaceful sleep.

Lizzie stirred. Her eyes opened and she sat up, wailing more gustily than before. Catherine took the little girl in her arms. Lizzie clung to Catherine as she had a month ago in the stream where they had first met. Again, Catherine felt a rush of fierce protectiveness toward the child.

"Hush, darling," she murmured.

Lizzie continued to sob, and Catherine wondered how to reach her.

"Lizzie, do you hear me? You are safe. I won't let the storm hurt you."

She was obliged to say it several times before Lizzie calmed down enough to respond.

"M—miss Catherine?" she said between sobs.

"Yes, it is I."

"The storm didn't take you away?"

"No, of course not."

Lizzie looked about nervously. "Where is Philip?"

"Here I am, Lizzie. We are all safe."

Catherine looked up, and saw him standing in the doorway, still fully dressed, although his cravat was slightly disordered.

"The storm didn't take anyone?" Lizzie asked.

"No, sweetheart," he said, taking a hesitant step into the room. Conscious of her own scanty attire, Catherine could see he was torn between the chivalrous urge to spare her embarrassment and the desire to comfort his sister.

"Why are you still dressed?" asked Lizzie.

"I could not sleep, sweetheart."

"Did the storm scare you?"

"No, it didn't."

"Why don't you come in?" Lizzie asked, beginning to look much more cheerful. "I won't be so afraid of the storm if you come in and cuddle with me and Miss Catherine."

"I can leave," said Catherine, and started to rise from the bed.

"No, please stay! I want *both* of you," said Lizzie, with a stubborn set to her little chin.

Philip looked at Catherine, a question in his eyes. Looking down into Lizzie's hopeful face, Catherine surrendered to the inevitable. She sat back down, putting her arm back around Lizzie.

In the candlelight, Philip's face looked a bit ruddy as he came in and sat carefully down on the other side of his sister, grimacing as the bed creaked under the added weight.

"Philip, you have to hold me, too."

Another questioning look from him, and again, Catherine nodded. Philip put his arm around them both; the strong, warm feel of his hand clasping her waist sparked a tingle of pleasure in her middle.

"There, is that better?" he asked his sister.

Lizzie nodded contentedly. For a moment, they all sat silently. Then Catherine realized the storm had abated.

"See, it is quiet now," said Philip. "The storm is gone. Do you think you will be able to sleep now?"

"First you must tell me how the water comes down at Lodore," said Lizzie.

"Must I?"

"Of course. Unless Miss Catherine wants to do it?"

"I'm not sure what you're asking, dear," she said.

"It's a poem by Mr. Southey, written to entertain his children," said Philip. "It is Lizzie's favorite."

"Well, I have never heard it, and I should like to."

"Oh, very well," he said, with a comic groan. Catherine realized this must be a frequent request of Lizzie's.

" 'How does the Water come down at Lodore?' " Philip began to recite. Catherine listened, savoring the sound of his voice as he described the progress of the water from its 'fountains in the mountains' down to the cataract at Lodore.

Lizzie listened attentively as the water went 'hurrying and skurrying, and thundering and floundering,' but as he went on, she began to relax. By the time the water was 'curling and purling and whirling and twirling,' Philip had softened his voice, and Lizzie was asleep leaning against him.

" 'And this way the Water comes down at Lodore,' " he ended in a whisper.

He exchanged glances with Catherine, and together they carefully let Lizzie back down onto the bed.

Catherine got up and found her candle. She left the room, conscious of Philip carrying his own candle, following close behind her.

In the hall, she turned to bid him good night and saw him looking down at her.

"Thank you for going to Lizzie," he whispered. "Ever since someone told her a storm claimed my parents' lives, she thinks that storms come to take people away. Dorothea says I overindulge her, but what else can I do but try to comfort her as best I can?"

She saw the worry in his face, and sensed for the first time how the burden of caring for his family pressed on him. He always seemed so strong and cheerful.

"Your family is lucky to have you," she whispered back. Impulsively, she took a step toward him, closing the short distance between them. He looked down in surprise as she stood on tiptoe, put her free arm around him, and kissed him.

Immediately, his muscular arm clasped her waist again, drawing her closer. Lips still joined, they clung together for a moment, as if frozen in a dance, both careful of the candles they were still holding. Then Philip deepened the kiss she had started. Her entire being tingled with the pleasure of it, and for a long, rapturous moment she allowed herself to slide into a realm of delight, where anything was possible.

Philip pulled his head back, and smiled down at her. There was such joy in his look Catherine felt pierced to the heart. Oh, she was wanton and cruel to encourage him, by kissing him so. And in her nightgown, no less!

"I'm so sorry! I didn't mean—I should not have kissed you," she said, making a feeble attempt to pull away from him again.

"There's no need to apologize, love. You may kiss me any time you wish," he said with a crooked smile. "Can you deny you have feelings for me *now?*"

"No, I cannot," she said helplessly, knowing only the truth would do now. "I do love you, Philip. But it's best we try to forget each other."

"Why? Whatever your trouble, surely we can overcome it together. Will you tell me what it is?"

Catherine's resolution wavered. What would it be like to share her concerns and joys with this man for the rest of her life? Was it not worth a try to find out if it was possible?

Hope and apprehension warred inside her. He deserved to know at least part of the truth. If he turned away from her because of it, she would have to bear the pain somehow. And if he did not . . .

She took a deep breath before giving him her answer.

"Yes. I will tell you."

Ten

"Let us go down to my study. It is too chilly here for us to talk."

Catherine could see how eager Philip was to hear her story, so she gathered her courage and turned to follow him down the corridor. They were probably safe from interruption. The servants were all asleep on the third floor, and it was unlikely that any of the family would awaken, as long as she and Philip were quiet. Softly, they went down the carpeted passageway and down the stairs. As her bare feet hit the ice-cold stone floor of the hall, Catherine winced, and involuntarily stepped back onto the last carpeted step.

"Give me your candle," Philip whispered.

She obeyed. He set both candles down on a table, then surprised a gasp out of her by picking her up. At first she stiffened, then leaned unresisting against his warm chest, her heart pounding furiously at the intimate contact, at the feel of his arms, one clasping her back, the other around her legs. With little apparent effort, he carried her across the hall toward his study, where she could see a fire still burning. Though a rug covered the floor, he did not set her down until he had reached a comfortable-looking chair by the fire.

She settled into the chair, trying to ignore the riotous feelings being clasped against his chest had in-

spired in her. She curled her feet under her and
wrapped the shawl around herself as discreetly as possible. If she invited any more lovemaking, she would
lose any shreds of judgment she still possessed.

She looked around as Philip put another log onto
the fire. She had never been in his study before. It was
a good-sized room. She was not surprised to see that
most of its walls were covered with bookshelves filled
nearly to overflowing. By now she knew that Philip's
parents had placed a greater importance on the education of their children than was customary for those of
their station in life. She knew Philip had studied at
Oxford and was a voracious reader of anything from
the classics to modern poetry.

She looked back at him, and watched as he stirred
the fire to a cheery blaze.

"Are you warm enough?" he asked, and she nodded.

"Perhaps you would care for a drink?" He walked
to a sideboard beyond his desk. From a decanter sitting there, he poured small amounts of golden liquid
into two glasses.

"What is it?"

"Uisge beatha," he intoned. "The water of life. I
got this while visiting a friend in Scotland."

"Do you think to loosen my tongue with it?" she
asked.

He smiled, handing her the glass. "Would that I
could. No, I only wish you to be comfortable."

He sat down in a chair on the other side of the fire
and drank his drink. Catherine gazed at the tiny
amount of amber-colored fluid in her glass, and took
a cautious sip. It seemed to burn her mouth, and all
the way down her throat.

"My, that is strong!" she said. She coughed, and felt a sudden rush of additional warmth course through her veins.

He grinned.

"I like it," she said, looking to see his reaction. "It is like fire, but it reminds me of flowers, too."

"It's heather you're tasting. This drink is made with water from the Highlands. We'll go there someday."

For just an instant, Catherine allowed herself to savor the spreading warmth from the drink, and dwell on the enticing image he had conjured up of their future life. Then she mentally shook herself. It was time she told Philip the truth. She set her glass down, and felt her mouth go suddenly dry with nervousness.

He was watching her silently, his expression grave. She could see he was afraid she would change her mind if he said anything more.

"Perhaps I should explain what happened the day we met," she began hesitantly. "I was trying to run away from my aunts."

"I'd guessed as much," he said.

She took a deep breath. "My father sent me to stay here, because I tried to elope with a gentleman of whom he disapproved. I wanted to get back to London, to try it again."

There. She had said it. She watched Philip's face for a reaction, but in the firelight it was difficult to read.

"And you were in love with this man?" he asked gruffly.

She knew there was no good answer to this question. She could see Philip was jealous, could hear it in his voice, but what would he think when he knew she had done such a scandalous thing without the excuse of true love?

"No, I was not," she replied after a pause.

"Why did you do it?"

"I wished to run away from my family."

"The ones who do not allow you to play your Beethoven," he said. "That can't have been the whole of it."

"No. My father had already chosen a suitor for me, a man I could not bear to marry."

"And so you tried to escape from an odious arranged marriage. Is that all?"

She could hear the relief in his voice. He should have been shocked; it would have been a merciful end to his feelings for her. But he was not, and she felt irrationally glad of it.

"Is that all?" he repeated softly.

She heard a hint of doubt creep into his voice, and winced inwardly. He was all too perceptive. Now was the time to tell him about the last Season, about Staverton. But she was weak; she could not do it.

"Isn't it enough?" she asked. "I nearly created a scandal. Do you wish your sisters to have such an example before them?"

She saw a crease in his forehead. Perhaps he suspected she still held something back, but he answered in a reassuring tone that warmed her to the heart.

"I shall never try to coerce my sisters into marriage. Certainly it was misguided of your father to do so. Perhaps he was only thinking of your well-being?"

Catherine shook her head. She couldn't tell Philip about the horrid choice her father had placed before her; he would never believe a parent would behave so.

"So your father sent you here in punishment, until such time that you would agree to marry the man of his choosing?"

"Yes, that was his plan," she said.

"You've made no other attempts to run away, though. Perhaps you've found your punishment less severe than intended?"

She could not help responding to the smile lurking in the depths of his eyes.

"At first, I stayed because I saw how upset my aunts were that I tried to run away. Of course, I would not think of distressing Aunt Phoebe," she said.

She thought she saw a curious look on his face, but he said nothing.

"Now I have other reasons . . ." She trailed off. She'd been about to say that she had stronger reasons for wishing to stay in Lynthwaite, but she felt her doubts returning. Philip had not been shocked by the tale of her attempted elopement; he had been warmly sympathetic. It still didn't solve other problems.

"So, you've found reasons to enjoy your stay here," he said. The smile in his eyes deepened as he got up. He came to kneel by her chair and took her hands in his. "Then marry me, Catherine. You've only to tell me your father's direction so I can ask him for your hand."

"It won't be as easy as that," she said. "My father will never give his permission."

"My family is an old and respected one; we've lived in this valley for almost two hundred years. I can support you in comfort, and even afford the occasional luxury. Don't you think he would approve?"

Her throat tightened at his earnest words. She could just imagine how *His Grace* would respond, when asked for her hand by a mere Mr. Philip Woodmere, of no title, modest wealth, and no social consequence to speak of. The duke's wrath would come down on him, on her, on Aunt Mattie and Aunt Phoebe, even on poor Ned and Jemima.

It was not as if His Grace truly cared what became of her. However, she felt certain he would not wish the world to think he had allowed her to marry a commoner of her own choosing. If he found out about her love for Philip, he was sure to whisk her away in short order, and shut her up at Whitgrave, or someplace more remote. It would be an end to everything, to all her chances for happiness, even the brief joy she was enjoying now.

"No!" she cried.

Philip looked startled at her vehemence.

"You don't think perhaps your mother might intercede for you?"

"My mother died the day I was born."

"I am sorry," he said, and tightened his grip on her hands in a simple gesture of sympathy.

"You are not one of the Arndales, are you, Catherine?" he asked after a moment. "Tell me, who is your father?"

"I cannot tell you," she said. "I promised Aunt Mattie I would not say, and I do not wish you to know."

"You should let me try," he said stubbornly.

"No, please don't!" she cried.

He released her hands, then got up and began to pace the room. Catherine felt tears spring to her eyes. She hated to anger him, but how could she explain?

"Good Lord, Catherine," he said, stopping in front of the fire. "I can't even elope with you if you won't tell me who you are!"

"You can't anyway! You cannot create such a scandal. Think of Marianne and Lizzie, and your brothers."

He looked at her, trouble in his eyes, and she could

see he knew she was right. He did not even know the half of it. If they eloped, he would be accused of seducing her for her fortune and aristocratic connections. She couldn't bring such a disaster upon him and his family.

He resumed his pacing, then paused by the window.

"You are right, we cannot elope. And you don't wish me to speak to your aunts or your father. You leave me very few choices."

Catherine thought her heart would burst. His voice was calm, resigned. It seemed he was on the verge of giving up. It was what she had intended, but it hurt nonetheless.

"How old are you?"

His abrupt question hung in the air for an instant, then she realized what he was asking.

"I am just turned nineteen."

Almost two whole years before she could marry as she pleased. It seemed an eternity.

"Jacob waited fourteen years to marry Rachel," he said. "I would rather wed you with your family's blessing, but I can wait two years if I must. Will you wait for me?"

She looked back at Philip. She saw the naked yearning in his eyes, the happiness he longed to offer her.

"If I can—if you still love me, I will marry you then."

He sighed, and returned to kneel at her side.

"Do you doubt my constancy?" he asked, taking her hands again. She loved the feel of his warm, hard grasp. When he touched her, she couldn't help hoping.

But two years, she thought, gazing into the fire. So much could happen in that time. Her father might try to take her back into the family, or he might discover their intentions and find some way to thwart them. Or more likely, she would spoil things herself, as she'd done in the past.

Still, if there was the slightest chance, she had to try to get it right this time.

"I don't doubt you," she said, with a shaky attempt at a smile.

"Then we *will* marry, sooner or later. It might be sooner, if you let me try. What harm could it do? If your father refuses his consent, we can wait if we must."

She shook her head.

"Don't you *wish* to marry me, Catherine?"

"I do," she said, wrung by the longing in his voice, and the appeal in his deep brown eyes. "But there's no knowing what my father might do to try to separate us. I can't take the chance."

"At least let me talk to your Aunt Matilda. I don't wish to be going behind her back, and I'm sure *she* will approve. Perhaps she can advise us."

Catherine thought this over for a moment. She hated to force Philip into anything he felt was wrong, or to lie to her aunts, for that matter. Aunt Mattie *did* like Philip; he was one of the few gentlemen of whom she approved wholeheartedly. She might prove a valuable ally, if only Catherine could convince her to help conceal their attachment.

"Very well," she said. "But let me speak to her first, please."

Philip's brows drew together, but to her relief, he nodded. He got up from the floor and stretched. "I think we should try to get some sleep now."

Catherine uncurled her legs and arose from her chair. Philip picked her up, and again she luxuriated in the wonderful sensation of being in his arms, and the feeling of being loved and cared for.

He carried her back through the chilly hall, and despite her hushed protest, up the stairs as well. Somehow he found his way through the dark passage until they reached her room. There, he set her down, still keeping his arms around her. She could barely see him, but raised her face instinctively for a lingering kiss that still ended far too soon.

Regretfully, Philip let Catherine go and held the door for her to go back into her room. He still couldn't quite believe she had agreed to marry him; he was conscious of a strong urge to keep holding her, for fear she might change her mind on leaving his arms.

He went to his room and prepared for sleep, now doubly glad that he'd sent his manservant off hours ago. He hadn't given up hoping to win Catherine's confidence, but tonight had exceeded all his dreams. True, she'd held some things back, but she'd made a start. She would tell him the rest when she was ready, he was sure of it.

Given her passionate nature, it was possible that she had developed an exaggerated notion of her father's opposition. Philip hoped she'd come to realize soon that she should let him approach her father.

He sighed. He longed to make Catherine his own, but if worst came to worst, he could be patient. He'd lived the life of a monk for years. Since a few youthful adventures during his days at Oxford, he hadn't so much as embraced a lady that was not his relation. He was not the sort of scoundrel who would seduce young ladies of his acquaintance, like the innocently frivolous Miss Cotterfields. Nor was it any part of a good landlord to dally with milkmaids, or the daughters of his tenants.

He had all a man's desires, nonetheless. It was not just a love of Nature that led him to take long, strenuous walks on the fells, at odd hours and in all sorts of weather. Still, it had been easier before he'd met Catherine. There had been no special woman who had aroused his desire. He hadn't *loved*.

On the bright side, at least he could enjoy Catherine's company, her music, and as many kisses as he could steal.

And he was going to be taking some very long walks.

Eleven

The next morning, Philip drove Catherine home in his phaeton. Their progress was slow due to the muddiness of the road, but the carriage was light and the horses fresh, so there was no danger of getting stuck. The occasional shower of mud kicked up by the pair was gradually bespattering the hem of Catherine's dress, but she didn't care a whit.

She had awoken that morning with a new sense of well-being that even the recollection of the challenges ahead could not stifle. Now she delighted in the fresh smell of the damp woods and fields, and the rushing and gurgling of the rain-swollen streams they crossed along the way.

She listened with interest as Philip told her more about members of his family she had yet to meet, his brother William in the navy, and his sister Jane, the one who had married the vicar of Little Hayfield in Derbyshire and had recently given birth to her first child.

Although he didn't question her, Catherine knew Philip hoped she would respond in kind. Much as she hated to disappoint him, she did not dare reveal any family details that might give away her identity. Sadly, she also realized that despite her aristocratic lineage, she had nothing very pleasant to relate about her own family.

Instead, she told Philip about Juliana and Penelope, and he laughed heartily at some of the stories she related about their school days. All too soon, they were within sight of Larkspur Cottage. As they drew near, Catherine saw Aunt Phoebe and Aunt Mattie both appear on the doorstep, shadowed by Ned and Jemima. Her optimistic mood ebbed at the sight of the latter two, a visible reminder of her father's influence.

"Are you sure you wish to speak with Miss Matilda alone?" Philip asked in a low voice.

She nodded.

"Tomorrow you must tell me what she has decided," he said, and pulled his horses up before the stone path leading to the cottage door. He helped her out, surreptitiously giving her a smile that made her feel as if she had just been kissed. Absurdly conscious of the onlookers, she thanked him before turning up the path.

Her aunts greeted her with the same relief and fond scolding they had shown her first morning with them. As soon as they were all alone in the sitting room, Catherine told her aunts that Philip had proposed, and that she had accepted.

"I have been hoping you two would make a match of it," said Aunt Phoebe, clapping her hands together. "Now you will be able to live close by, always. Isn't it delightful, Mattie?"

"Hmph," said Aunt Matilda, looking thoughtful. "It depends."

"Oh, don't be such a wet blanket!" cried Aunt Phoebe. "Depends on what, pray tell?"

"On their reasons for marrying, of course. Do not

forget, Phoebe, Catherine was sent here because she was on the verge of eloping with a veritable scoundrel."

"Oh, but our dear Mr. Woodmere is just the man to replace him in her affections. Isn't that just what he did, dear?"

"I never think of Verwood anymore," Catherine concurred, with perfect truth. How foolish and impulsive she had been to think of eloping with him!

"See, Mattie?" said Aunt Phoebe triumphantly. "All is well now."

"How you do rush on, Phoebe!" Aunt Mattie said, then looked sharply at Catherine. "We are quiet folk here in the valley. You seem to have enjoyed your time with us, Catherine, but do you think you will be happy spending the rest of your life here?"

"Yes," she replied without hesitation. "This is more my home than any place I have ever been."

"Mr. Woodmere has serious obligations to his brothers and sisters. Are you prepared to act as a mother to them?"

These words gave Catherine pause. She thought of the younger Woodmeres, and realized that they had wrapped themselves around her heart almost as strongly as Philip had. She longed to help him raise them, to share the responsibilities he had shouldered so patiently since his parents' death. However, she was woefully conscious that nothing in her life had prepared her for such a role.

"I shall try my best," she said.

"Good. I am happy to see you showing such good sense, Catherine," Aunt Mattie said. She still looked concerned. "Unfortunately, it will be a difficult task to convince your father of that. I am afraid Mr. Woodmere has neither the family connections nor the wealth to impress him."

"How can you say so, Mattie? The Woodmeres are an old and respected family. Dear Mr. Woodmere owns half the land hereabouts, besides an interest in a quarry over on Kirkby Moor. Not to mention the Woodmeres have one closed carriage, and two open!"

"Do not be a widgeon, Phoebe!" said Aunt Matilda. "The duke probably owns a dozen carriages of his own. I am sure he wishes Catherine to marry a lord."

"A marquess, as a matter of fact," said Catherine.

Both her aunts looked at her questioningly.

"My father did not tell you that?" she asked. "When he sent me here, he gave me a choice. I could live here indefinitely, or accept an offer from the Marquess of Hornsby. A man old enough to be my grandfather!"

Her aunts exchanged shocked glances.

"It is worse than I thought," said Aunt Matilda. "If you wish, Catherine, I will do my best to persuade the duke to approve Mr. Woodmere's suit."

"No, please! That is not what I want."

"Then what *do* you want?"

"For you to help keep our secret. I have not even told Mr. Woodmere who my father is. I don't want him going to ask for my hand. You know His Grace would have me away from here in the twinkling of an eye if he knew I loved such a man. He would do his best to find a way to keep us apart permanently. I cannot take the risk; I would rather wait two years to marry."

Aunt Phoebe looked distressed, and even Aunt Mattie appeared to be moved. However, she shook her head, saying, "I do not like secrets. The irritating things have a way of coming out."

Catherine looked at her, pleading with her eyes.

Aunt Mattie relented. "No doubt I shall regret this, but very well, Catherine. We will keep your secret, at least for a few months. Your father may be more amenable to Mr. Woodmere's suit if he has had time to give up hope of this doddering marquess."

"Thank you so much, both of you," she said, smiling at her aunts.

"Mattie, do you think perhaps it is time we revealed our little secret as well?" said Aunt Phoebe, looking hopefully at her sister.

Aunt Mattie inclined her head. "Dear Catherine, Phoebe and I do have a confession to make."

Catherine stared at Aunt Phoebe, whose face had turned pink with embarrassment.

"What is it, dear aunt?"

"Well, I am—I am not—Oh, I hope you will not be angry with me for this—"

"I promise you I will not," said Catherine, wondering at the cause of Aunt Phoebe's agitation.

"What Phoebe is trying to tell you, Catherine, is that she is perfectly healthy," said Aunt Mattie. "She does not have a weak heart. We have been pretending."

"Whatever for?" she asked, confused for an instant. "Oh, it was a ruse to keep me from running away again, was it not?"

"I do hope you are not angry with us, dear!" said Aunt Phoebe.

Even Aunt Mattie looked anxious. Catherine felt a gurgle of laughter rise in her throat.

"No, not at all! How could I be? If you had not persuaded me to stay, I should not have gotten to know Philip!"

"I am glad you see it that way," said Aunt Mattie.

"Now I shall be able to enjoy some hill-walking again!" said Aunt Phoebe, jumping up from her seat with an ecstatic smile. "Shall we all go for a ramble now? It is *such* a lovely day!"

"We will all be plastered with mud," said Aunt Mattie, frowning but with a twinkle in her eye nevertheless. "But very well. Catherine, remember to put on your stoutest boots."

As they all got up to leave the sitting room, Catherine took the opportunity to thank her aunts again. She embraced Aunt Mattie first, and was shocked to see a tear on her formidable aunt's cheek.

"You are a good girl, Catherine," said Aunt Mattie gruffly. "I hope you will be happy."

Catherine smiled wistfully as she turned to Aunt Phoebe. She knew she would be happy. The only question was, for how long?

Over the following month, Philip had few opportunities to be alone with Catherine. Though they saw each other almost every day, it was almost always in company of her aunts or his family. Sometimes it irked him, but it was an idyllic period nevertheless.

As May turned to June, the finer weather lured Philip and his family into all sorts of outdoor activities, from the practical to the purely frivolous. Catherine delighted in the annual sheep-washing, laughing merrily at the sight of him helping to wrestle the silly beasts into the stream. She accompanied him and his brothers and sisters on several pleasure excursions. They climbed up Druid's Hill to fly kites, and went boating on Ullswater, where Catherine earned Harry and Jack's undying respect by fishing with them and showing not even a hint of feminine squeamishness.

Most days, she came to Woodmere Hall to teach Marianne and Lizzie, and to fill the house with the most enchanting music. She often cajoled Philip into singing for her, and accompanied him on the pianoforte. He'd always enjoyed music, but now it was a special pleasure, an intimacy they could safely share.

On the few precious occasions when they were alone, he managed to steal a few kisses. Gradually, she seemed to be losing her earlier restraint, responding to his embraces with an ever-increasing passion that played havoc with all his virtuous resolutions.

More disturbing was the look he caught on her face during some of their happiest moments: a singular look of rapture mingled with sadness. He had the strange feeling she was storing up memories of these days to treasure later, as if she did not share his certainty that there would be many more of the same.

As for him, he was more convinced than ever that fate had brought him and Catherine together for a reason. Whatever barriers existed between them, real or imagined, they would overcome them in time.

She had rarely felt such a glow of anticipation, Catherine thought as she watched Philip come forward to help her into his phaeton. It was a glorious summer afternoon. There was not a cloud in the vivid blue sky, and she and Philip would be together alone for the entire drive to Keswick.

Behind them, the Woodmeres' coach followed, carrying her great-aunts, Miss Dorothea and Marianne, who was all agog at the prospect of her very first assembly. At the outlet of the valley they would be joined by three more coaches, carrying the Maldons and the Cotterfields. Philip had asked her aunts if he could drive Catherine in the phaeton, so that she might better enjoy the new sights they would pass. To her delight, they had agreed.

Philip smiled at her warmly as he helped her into the carriage, then took up the reins. Settling back in the seat, she prepared for the pleasant torture it was to sit so close to him and not be able to touch him or be touched by him, other than the occasional brush of leg against leg caused by the motion of the carriage. With the drivers of the other carriages in sight, Philip would not be able to so much as put an arm around her waist, but at least they would be able to talk, and enjoy the scenery together in a rare spell of privacy.

"Ah, this is lovely," he said, as if reading her thoughts. "I have you all to myself. I'm tempted not to go to Keswick at all. Perhaps we should head toward the border instead, love?"

She smiled at his joke, but shook her head.

"Sometimes I do wish we could run off together," he said, sighing. "You know how I long for you, Catherine. Won't you show some mercy? I might fall into a decline if I have to wait too long."

"If you fall into a decline, I promise to nurse you most devotedly."

She chuckled at the thought of her rugged Corsair lounging around on a sofa, surrounded by pills and potions. She also felt more than a twinge of guilt. There was a steadfast purpose behind his funning. It was his way of letting her know he continued to hope that she would permit him to approach her father about marrying her. She sensed that beneath the humor, he was hurt by her continued refusal to do so. The dangerous thing was, she was more and more tempted to tell him. She reminded herself that it was folly to believe her father would relent. It was better to suffer the torment of waiting than risk being parted from Philip, perhaps forever.

She changed the subject, telling him how pleased Ned and Jemima had been at being given a holiday from their usual tasks. Obligingly, Philip followed her lead and corroborated her happy suspicion that her one-time guards had conceived a pronounced fondness for each other's company.

They chatted at random for a few miles. Soon they reached Troutbeck and drove on, admiring the views of Blencathra as they progressed to the picturesque Vale of St. John. They stopped, along with the others, to explore the famous stone circle at Castlerigg. Although the ring was beautifully situated and larger than the one on the Woodmeres' land, Catherine decided Philip's stone circle would always hold the greater spell over her.

After about half an hour, they rejoined the main road and continued to progress toward Keswick. Soon they were within sight of the modest town, nestling between the north end of Derwentwater and the southern slopes of Skiddaw, one of highest mountains in all the Lakes. Catherine gazed up at the lofty summit in awe. Although she knew the Alps were much higher, she had never seen anything so magnificent herself.

"We shall climb it together one day," said Philip, smiling at her enthusiasm.

Her heart skipped a beat at the thought, and not merely because she longed to make the ascent with

Philip. It was just that the future he envisioned for them suddenly seemed so precious, and so real.

Almost too quickly, their little cavalcade arrived at the Queen's Head, the inn where the assembly was to be held, and where they would spend the night before returning to Lynthwaite on the morrow. Most of the party went for a walk before dinner. Although she could no longer be private with Philip, Catherine found Derwentwater delightful. It was pleasant to stroll along its lightly wooded shores, to view its assortment of small, jewel-like islands, and watch the sun slowly descending over the surrounding fells.

They returned to the inn to dress, then rejoined in the private parlor, where they would enjoy a late dinner before the start of the assembly. Catherine had dressed with especial care, glad that Mariah had packed all her gowns for her stay in Cumberland. She had never expected she would have an opportunity to wear this one: an elegantly simple white satin with a low bodice in a contrasting rose color. She hoped Philip would enjoy the sight of her wearing it.

His reaction when he looked up and saw her was all she could have wished for. He gave her one smoldering glance, then looked away. Suddenly she longed to be alone with him again, longed for a time when it would not be necessary to hide the strength of their attachment from everyone.

At least she could look forward to their first dance.

After dinner, Catherine and the rest of the party made their way to the assembly room that had been built along one side of the inn. At the door, they were cordially greeted by the innkeeper, in his role as master of ceremonies. He pointed out doors along one side of the room that led to a card room and a tearoom, respectively. The assembly room itself was large and sparsely furnished with only a few wooden chairs along the walls, which were covered with a simple striped wallpaper. At one end of the room, musicians were tuning their instruments; nearer the doorway, a few groups of festively clad ladies and gentlemen awaited the start of the dancing.

Catherine chuckled inwardly at the contrast between this humble setting and the ballrooms she had previously danced in, with their gilt mirrors and opulent decorations. She reflected that the duke and duchess would never have permitted her to attend this sort of affair, where anyone with the modest price of admission could attend.

The thought only added to her delight in the occasion.

Philip led their group toward some chairs along one side of the room, where the older members of their party could watch the dancing. As they passed one of the other groups, Catherine could not help overhearing a snatch of their conversation.

"Just fancy! A lord and his new wife are staying at this very inn!" one lady said, fluttering her fan excitedly.

"Oh, do you think they will condescend to make an appearance here?" asked her companion.

Catherine could not make out any more, but it was enough to make her wish she had never come. A lord and lady staying here? What if they knew her?

Then she told herself she was worrying too much. The aristocratic couple might not deign to attend this humble assembly, and if they did, it was unlikely that they would recognize her. Any members of the *haut ton* she was acquainted with would still be in London at this season.

After seating her great-aunts, Philip claimed Catherine's hand for the first dance. Along with the other members of the group, they joined the first set. The music began, and she soon discovered that despite his size, Philip moved quickly and gracefully, and took a robust pleasure in the lively country dance.

Out of the corner of her eye, she saw with delight that Charlotte was dancing with Captain Maldon, who was smiling down at his partner with obvious affection. Charlotte looked quite radiant, in a becoming pale green gown of Catherine's which Grimsby had altered with surprising skill. However, Catherine knew that it was not her modish new attire that brought the bloom to Charlotte's cheeks.

To Catherine's other side, Marianne danced with Charles Cotterfield. Philip's sister looked perfectly adorable in her white muslin trimmed with blue ribbons, and Catherine was not at all surprised to see young Cotterfield looking quite smitten. Perhaps in time their youthful infatuation might mature into something more. At any rate, it had been wise of Philip not to have made any overly autocratic moves to put a halt to it.

The figures of the dance brought her into contact with both Captain Maldon and Mr. Cotterfield, and Catherine smiled at them both, but secretly longed to be rejoined with Philip. Whenever his strong hand grasped her gloved one, she felt a singular, sweet thrill even from the slight contact. When she looked into his face, she could see her own desire mirrored in his eyes.

She wondered how long they could continue this restraint. How long their desire could be solaced by the mere touch of a hand, the rare stolen kiss? Again, she was tempted to give in to Philip's arguments, and permit him to approach her father, but she knew that was folly. No, she had best try to be satisfied with these simple pleasures, rather than ruin everything by wishing for more.

With renewed vigor, she threw herself into the dance. She and Philip joined hands and ducked under the linked arms of Charlotte and Captain Maldon, going in the direction of the doorway. Then she straightened, looked up, and stumbled.

There, in the doorway, being greeted by the obsequious master of ceremonies, stood the last person she would have expected, or wished to see here. Adrian Denham, Viscount Staverton, heir to the earldom of Prestbury.

The man she had once hoped to marry.

"Is something amiss?" Philip asked, steadying her.

She recovered and shook her head as she moved back into place. Quickly she glanced toward the doorway, and her worst fears were realized. Staverton had seen her; in fact, he was staring at her, his mouth slightly agape. Beside him stood a short, plump lady with yellow curls, dressed in the height of fashion but sporting a disdainful expression. Feeling as if she'd been dealt a double blow, Catherine recognized her old nemesis. Lydia Bixley, leader of the catty set at Miss Stratton's, an incurable gossip and a sanctimonious talebearer. So that was the lady Staverton had married!

Meanwhile, Catherine forced herself to concentrate on the remaining figures of the dance, as Philip watched her, looking concerned. She could not say anything to him amongst such a crowd, so she glanced

again toward the Stavertons, then back at Philip, trying
to convey a silent warning along with a plea for his
trust.

With a sinking heart, she saw the Stavertons move
into the room and come to stand quite near where her
great-aunts, Miss Woodmere, and the older Cotterfields were all sitting. There was no way she could
avoid meeting them, although she felt sick at the prospect. Of all the ways Philip might learn about her family and her past, this was the most ruinous.

The dance ended, and Philip offered her his arm to
escort her back to her aunts. She laid her hand over it,
agonized that it might be the last time they touched so.
She did not know how he would react to the news that
her father was a duke. Even more harrowing was the
thought of what Staverton and Lydia might say about
her last Season.

"Dearest Kitty!" shrieked Lydia as they approached.
Catherine stiffened. She hated being called Kitty, and
Lydia knew it. There was a predatory light in Lydia's
eyes; Catherine realized she was deliberately being
baited.

"Or should I say Lady Catherine?" Lydia continued,
in an arch manner that made Catherine wish she could
slap her. "We were *such* friends at Miss Stratton's I
don't know why we should not dispense with such for-
malities!"

Catherine felt Philip's arm tense under her hand.
"Lady Catherine?" he asked, doubt and shock in his
voice.

"What?" asked Lydia, staring at them both. "You
have been dancing with Lady Catherine Harcourt,
daughter of His Grace the Duke of Whitgrave, and
didn't even know it?" She tittered, and Catherine felt

nearly sick with anger and apprehension of what was to follow.

Philip turned to look at her, an aching question in his eyes. She felt painfully conscious that he had taken a step back from her, and that everyone in her own party had fallen silent and were watching her with rampant curiosity or dread.

"Yes, I am Lady Catherine Harcourt," she said, realizing as she did how much she loathed the name and all it meant.

She could hardly bear to look at Philip. His face was rigidly impassive, but his eyes cried out to her. She could see, as clearly as if he'd voiced it, his anger and hurt at discovering the truth in such a manner. She gazed back into his eyes, imploring his understanding and forgiveness. The anger in his face faded, but was replaced by a troubled expression. She could see he was just coming to realize the gulf between their social stations, and the true magnitude of the obstacles that lay in their path.

She wished she could be alone with him somewhere where no one else could disturb their happiness. But that was impossible. Suddenly coming back to a sense of her surroundings, Catherine realized everyone was still staring at her: her great-aunts, with anxious expressions, the others of their party, still looking stunned, and the Stavertons, both eyeing her with unbridled curiosity.

Good heavens! Had they seen the glances she'd just exchanged with Philip? She didn't want to think about what conclusions they might draw, and what they might do about it.

She pulled herself together, and made the necessary introductions, forcing herself to keep her voice light and casual when introducing Philip and his family. His face was totally impassive now; she wished she knew what he was thinking. She could only hope that he had understood how important it was to hide their attachment from the Stavertons.

As soon as Catherine had completed the introductions, Aunt Mattie came forward. In her most dignified manner she addressed herself to Lord and Lady Staverton.

"My niece has been living with us as Miss Arndale, to escape the unwanted attention her rank would otherwise attract. I am certain both of you will respect her wishes and not spread word of her presence or identity further."

"Of course not. We won't breathe a word, will we, Stavie?" said Lydia, turning to her husband.

He nodded, looking embarrassed. Catherine noticed now that his face was flushed, his blond locks were a trifle disordered, and there was a wild, unfocused look in his eyes. Had he perhaps overindulged in his wine at dinner?

She looked back at Aunt Mattie, grateful for her attempt to explain the awkward situation. Perhaps if they all just spoke politely for a few more minutes, the Stavertons would leave them alone. She forced herself to listen to Lydia's babbling, and realized Lydia was speaking of her family.

"I hear the duke and duchess have already returned to Whitgrave, and are entertaining a most exalted set of guests there. Am I right in supposing that we shall soon hear a most Interesting Announcement?"

Catherine looked at Lydia blankly.

"What, you do not know?" Lydia giggled again. "Well, I shall tell you. Among the visitors at Whitgrave are the Earl of Ibstone and his mother. Your charming sister has succeeded in attracting the most eligible of suitors! Oh, I would envy Lady Susannah quite desperately, were it not that dear Stavie here is also heir to an earldom!"

Lydia fluttered her eyelashes at Staverton, who not only seemed oblivious, but continued to stare at Catherine with something like hunger in his eyes. Catherine could not understand it; he had been the one who had ended things last Season, not she.

But this was no time to indulge in speculation. She forced a smile to her lips and said, "I have been remiss in offering my felicitations on your own marriage. How long have you been married?"

"Thank you so much, dearest Kitty! We are on our honeymoon trip. Darling Stavie was so impatient to wed me that he just could not wait for the end of the Season. Is that not right, my lord?" she asked, with a simpering look at her husband.

"Quite right, dear," he muttered.

"It is a wonderful thing to inspire such *lasting* affection in a man," said Lydia soulfully.

Catherine realized from Lydia's victorious smile that she hoped to make her jealous. It was ridiculous. Looking at Staverton, Catherine realized that though he was as handsome as she remembered, she had long ago lost any final shreds of affection she had had for him.

Still, he was a painful reminder of what had happened last Season. She wished he would stop leering at her so, but it was the wine, no doubt. She had never seen him in his cups before.

"Shall we dance, Lady Catherine?" he asked, slurring his words slightly.

Catherine started in surprise, then instinctively looked at Philip. His expression was carefully stoic, but she could still see the turmoil in his eyes. She knew he was waiting with bated breath to see how she would answer.

She looked back at Staverton, hoping he and Lydia hadn't noticed her looking at Philip again. She couldn't decide whether refusing or casually accepting the invitation would seem less suspicious to everyone involved.

"Please? For old times' sake," Staverton pleaded, with an odd look of desperation in his eyes. She couldn't imagine why he wished to dance with her, when their last dance together had ended so disastrously.

Lydia looked daggers at her husband. "Stavie love, can you not see Kitty prefers *not* to dance with you? You would not wish to cause her pain, would you?"

Catherine bit her lip. In her stupid, jealous way Lydia was making a terrible stir over this one dance. Catherine didn't know what to do. How could she convince everyone that she no longer cherished any feelings for Staverton, but at the same time hide her affection for Philip?

"Nonsense, Lydia," she replied, striving to appear totally indifferent. "I should be delighted to dance with Staverton. That is, if you feel you can trust your husband to dance with other ladies?"

Lydia's eyes shot venom at Catherine, but mercifully she was at a loss for a reply.

As Staverton led Catherine away from the group, she repressed the urge to look back over her shoulder at Philip. Perhaps he would understand what she was trying to do; or perhaps he was jealous. All she could do was try to behave with cool dignity until she could be alone with him and try somehow to explain everything.

She followed Staverton to the center of the floor. Suddenly, she realized that the floor was empty save for the two of them, and that the musicians were playing a waltz. She looked up at Staverton in surprise, and saw a self-satisfied smile on his face.

"I asked the master of ceremonies if they could play a waltz, and he was more than happy to oblige," he said. "Of course, I did not know then that I would be dancing with *you.*"

He took her hand in one of his, and placed his other on her waist. She flinched inwardly, and wished she could break free. But that would cause even more of a sensation than the sight of them waltzing in this rural town, so she forced herself to tolerate his touch and follow his lead.

It didn't help that no one else was dancing. It was no wonder, for the waltz was such a new dance that no one in such a remote district knew how to perform it. She was horridly conscious of shocked stares from the onlookers, and of Philip. His expression was carefully controlled but his watchful eyes and his stance betrayed the torment she was causing him.

"Why did you ask me to dance, Staverton?" she asked abruptly.

"Last Season, you called me Adrian," he said, with something like a pout.

"I did many foolish things last Season. I repeat, why did you ask me to dance?"

"I am sorry," he said. "I suppose you must hate me. I had thought I'd forgotten you, but then I saw you, and could not rest until we had talked once more.

"You have a wife to talk to now."

"Lydia doesn't—how shall I explain?" He paused, looking embarrassed again. "Lydia and I married rather suddenly. She—er, I—we were caught in a—a compromising position. That's why we came to this curst, godforsaken place. I couldn't bear the way everyone was laughing at me, for falling victim to such a trap. I wish I'd never done it!"

"I do not know what any of this has to do with me."

"Don't be so cruel! You don't know how I am suffering. The damned chit hasn't shown me a scrap of affection since! Not in private, anyway. On our wedding night, she—she told me she knew it was her duty to produce an heir, and just to—to get *on* with it. I wish I had married you instead!"

"I am so glad you did not realize that last year; I would have been fool enough to marry you then!"

"Don't be so cold, Catherine! I—"

"Don't call me Catherine! You have made your bed; you must lie in it now. Why should I care about your troubles? It is very wrong of you to discuss them with me."

"No, it isn't. I want *you.*"

He leaned forward toward her. Catherine smelled the wine on his breath, and realized he was even more drunk than she had thought. It was a relief when the steps dictated he release her temporarily.

"No, you do not!" she said, wondering when those blasted musicians would stop their playing so she could return to her aunts.

Staverton pulled her back in toward him, and twirled her around, holding her much more closely than was proper.

"But I do want you. There's a back door at the end

of the corridor," he said in a low, urgent voice. She prayed no one heard it over the music. "It leads to the garden," he continued. "I'll make an excuse to slip away for a moment, and you can do the same."

She faltered in her steps and stared at him. Good God! Could he really be asking her to sport with him in the garden?

"You are drunk, and you are insulting," she said. "I would slap you if I did not care about embarrassing my aunts."

"You must help me," he said, pulling her back into the rhythm of the dance. "I *need* you. Why won't you come with me? You are not worrying about Lydia? You don't like her, do you?"

"That is not the point!"

"I see. You're infatuated with that hulking brute you were dancing with, aren't you?" he said in a peevish tone.

"I don't know what you are talking about. Mr. Woodmere is nothing to me," she said in a carefully airy voice. Inwardly, her heart ached. She didn't know if she felt worse about denying her love for Philip, or because she feared she couldn't fool Staverton.

"Don't lie to me. I saw the way you were looking at him! Your father thinks you are living in modest seclusion, but you've taken the opportunity to dally with a country squire instead, haven't you?"

He looked her over knowingly, eyes resting on her décolletage. She felt smirched by his gaze. She'd never guessed he was such a spoilt puppy, or that he had such a low, base mind.

"I won't tell your father about your precious yokel, if you'll just let me sample some of what you're giving him," he said, with a leer.

She stared at him in disgust and rising horror. She couldn't do what he asked; she couldn't do anything to stop him from ruining everything.

She tried to twist away from him, but he held her hand tightly. An instant later, she felt his hand on her back again.

"Catherine, you're driving me mad," he said, rubbing his hand suggestively over her back. "I can pleasure you better than this bumpkin of yours. You enjoyed my little attentions last Season; now, we can do so much more!"

Rage and despair rose in her stomach in a nauseating, wounding spiral. She could bear it no longer. This time, she succeeded in breaking free from Staverton's grasp. At the same moment, she saw Philip crossing the room, fists clenched.

How she hated Staverton for bringing matters to such a crisis! But even more, she hated herself. In the end, it was her fault Philip was enduring this torture.

She couldn't bear to face him either.

Turning, she ran toward the doorway, into the inn's front room, and out into the night.

Twelve

Ignoring the shouts of several waiting coachmen, Catherine ran out of the town, back toward the lake. She had to get away, to find a spot somewhere out in the cool darkness of the night where she could be alone.

She heard Philip's voice call her name in the distance. Choking down a sob, she ran on, until she reached the trees by the lakeside. She leaned against one of them, trying to catch her breath. Perhaps she could hide here for a while, and collect herself before rejoining everyone again.

"Catherine!"

Philip's voice was louder than before. He sounded desperately anxious; it was cruel to worry him so.

She stepped out of the cover of the trees to meet him.

"There you are!"

She could hear the relief in his voice, see it in his face as he approached, at a run. She would have preferred his anger; it would have made her next task easier.

He tried to take her into his arms, but she evaded his embrace.

"Please leave me be!" she cried, wrapping her arms around herself.

He stepped back, as if she had struck him.

"Why did you run away from me, Catherine?" he asked roughly.

"I can't explain!"

"You must," he said. "If there is any hope for us, you must tell me what is going on."

"There is no hope for us."

"I won't believe that!"

She looked down, heart wrung by the vehemence in his voice. "You know who my father is now."

"The devil fly away with your father! We'll solve that problem when we come to it. I want to know about Staverton. What is he to you?"

"Nothing! Less than nothing!"

"Then why has he upset you so? Why did you dance with him?"

"I did not want him to guess about *us*. I thought that if I appeared totally unconcerned, he and Lydia might go away and not trouble us anymore."

He sighed. "I hoped it was that. When I first saw him put his hand on you, I felt like killing him on the spot. Then his wife informed us that this new dance was all the rage in London. If you knew how I felt, standing there, watching the two of you, unsure of what you were doing, unable to stop it . . . But when that miserable popinjay started pawing you, I could bear it no longer. You know I would have protected you. Why did you run away?"

He was angry and hurt, but how could she answer? She couldn't tell him about the threats Adrian had made, the choice he had offered her. It was too shameful, too sordid to repeat. She began to tremble with shock from all that had happened, and heard a swish of cloth behind her. An instant later, Philip draped his coat about her shoulders.

"Miss Matilda is waiting on a bench, back at the head of the lake," he said, more gently. Turning her head, Catherine saw her aunt in the distance. "She has given me leave to talk to you for a while, then we can all return together. Come, Catherine. Let us walk together. The time for secrets is past."

She nodded, thinking it was so like him to set aside his hurt and envelop her in warmth, to have such a care for her reputation. A lump rose in her throat at the thought of his kindness. She didn't deserve it. What *he* deserved was the truth. In a way, it would be a relief to tell him, and get the pain over and done with.

He put an arm around her shoulders, and they began to walk along the lake. A three-quarter moon shed its bright light over the scene; a myriad stars were reflected on the mysterious surface of the lake. Silence enveloped them, broken only by the soft lapping of wavelets against the shore. All was serene and romantic, heartbreakingly beautiful.

She sighed and began her tale. "I met Lord Staverton for the first time last spring, at a ball in London. Soon he became my most ardent suitor, or so I thought. He told me he was going to seek my father's permission to pay his addresses to me, but he did not come when he said he would. I wondered and worried for perhaps a week, then I saw him at another ball. He asked me to dance, and when I begged him to explain what had happened, he told me he had had a change of heart. I ran off, leaving him alone. My family have never forgiven me the scandal I created."

"How could they blame *you?* It seems to me it was

Staverton's fault. Why are you still so upset over it? Surely you don't still care for him?"

"No. I thought I loved him, but I never did." She looked down, overcome with shame as she remembered just how easily she had fooled herself.

"Don't be so overwrought, love. Everyone makes mistakes; just be glad you didn't marry that stupid fribble. By the way, why did he change his mind? From what I saw back there he still finds you irresistible."

There. It had come. The question she had been dreading. But it was past time for evasions.

"He told me I was too . . . *passionate*," she replied in a low voice.

She was startled to hear a rumble of laughter. "What a damned fool he is! Catherine, your passion is one of the reasons I love you so much. So many live their lives without caring, without truly feeling. Do you know I was ready to do the same, to order my life by expedience and practicality alone. Then I met you. I thank God for that day!"

He hadn't understood! She had to find another way to explain what Staverton had meant. Even if it felt like wrenching her own heart out. She was still trying to find the right words, when they passed into another small grove of trees. In their shadow, Philip stopped, turned her toward him, and pulled her into his arms. She told herself she should push him away, and tell him the truth, that last Season she had allowed—no, not merely allowed, but wantonly invited Staverton's attentions. That this Season she had all intentions of doing the same with Verwood.

And she had not been in love with either of them.

Then Philip began to kiss her, as he had never done

before, with a fierce possessiveness born, no doubt, from everything he had just endured. She took a shaky step backward, and felt her back press against a tree trunk. Philip came in closer, as if trying to meld her body into his. She felt his warm breath upon her as he ravished her mouth, then moved to her cheek, her throat, and the sensitive place under her ear.

She held her breath, trying to gather the resolution to stop him. She didn't deserve this honorable, loving man's ardor. But she was powerless . . . weak . . . wanton, and she could not do it. She entwined her arms around him and gave herself up to his embrace. He kissed her on the lips again, and this time she parted them willingly, welcoming him in, matching his fierce hunger.

A wild, sweet rapture took hold of her as he raised a hand to caress her through the delicate satin of her bodice. She gasped with pleasure, and he broke their kiss once more to taste her ear, her throat, her shoulder. Helplessly, she reveled in his attentions, twining one arm around his waist, lifting the other to stroke the dark locks that brushed the top of her shoulder. Through the intoxication of his lovemaking, one joyous thought echoed through her being. He still loved her.

God help her, she couldn't give him up!

"Cathy, my Cathy," he said in a hoarse voice. No one had called her that since childhood, and the simple endearment smote her to the core. Relaxing his hold, Philip lifted a hand to brush the tears from her cheek, and she wondered when she had begun to weep.

"Don't cry, love," he said. "I'll admit we're in a devilish coil, but it will all end well. I promise you."

She leaned her head into his chest, feeling the

strong beat of his heart beneath his fine linen shirt and silk waistcoat. Her own heart lifted at the confidence in his voice, and she made a vow. If she could not give him up, at least she would never hurt him. She would never let him know he had not been the first to awaken her passion, as Staverton had called it.

The thought of Staverton jerked her out of her brief sense of hopefulness.

"I wish I could believe you," she said, looking back up at him. "I failed us tonight. I have angered both Staverton and Lydia, and they will take their revenge by sending word to my father."

"It doesn't matter," he said. In the moonlight, she saw a defiant glint in his eye. "I'm going to arrange my affairs tomorrow so that I can talk to your father myself, before any tattling letter of theirs can reach him."

"I wish you would not go!" she said, full of dread at the thought of the reception he would receive at Whitgrave.

"I must," he replied, as she knew he would. "I know your father won't think me good enough for you—"

"You are too good for me!" she interrupted hotly.

"As I was saying, love, I know your father won't think me good enough, but even if he refuses at first, I should be able to convince him in time. I can stay with Jane and Robert until I do."

She was silent now, knowing it would do no good to try to dissuade him. His plan was the only chance they had, now that she had been found out.

"Come, it is time we returned to your aunt," he said. He rearranged his coat around her shoulders and turned back toward Keswick. Reluctantly, she went along with him toward where Aunt Mattie sat awaiting them.

As they walked, Philip sighed. "And here I'd been thinking we'd come out for a mere night of dancing. By the way, if you ever wish to waltz again, you must teach me how, for I'll not let you dance it with anyone else!"

She smiled, knowing he was trying lighten her mood. "I'm so sorry! I never meant for you to endure anything like this evening. I am afraid there are worse troubles ahead."

"Don't look so worried, love. I *will* prevail on your father, if I have to storm that damned castle to do it!"

Three days later, Philip came to the conclusion that storming the castle would have been far preferable to the interminable wait he had been put through. He paced across the richly carpeted floor of the library, where he'd been directed at Whitgrave Castle, his impatience rising.

Yesterday, he'd not gotten even this far; he'd been informed that His Grace was not at home to visitors. Today, the duke was closeted in his study with an architect, going over plans for building a new folly on the castle grounds. Philip had been told that the duke would condescend to see him if time remained after his more important business was concluded.

Finally, he was admitted into the study, where His Grace the Duke of Whitgrave sat in a mahogany chair behind a desk of the same exotic wood, sharpening a pen with a look of intense concentration.

"Good day, Your Grace," Philip said with a bow.

The duke continued to sharpen his quill, without looking up, without offering him a seat.

Philip had been prepared for a cool reception, but he had not expected such studied rudeness from a duke. He would have thought His Grace would be above such paltry behavior, but then he remembered what Jane had told him about the man. According to Jane, Catherine's father had come into the title unexpectedly, when an illness had decimated the main branch of the family. He was a man of modest ability, and had never managed to win the respect or the affection of his dependents, as the earlier dukes had done. Perhaps his inordinate consciousness of his rank sprang from an innate sense of unworthiness.

It still didn't excuse his rudeness, or his harsh treatment of his daughter.

Philip studied the duke curiously, but could find no family resemblance to Catherine. His Grace was of medium height, a little stout, with graying blond hair receding from a pallid, thin-skinned face that looked as if it reddened easily. His eyes were blue, but small and pale where Catherine's were large and full of light.

Philip remembered the way she had looked, the way she had clung to him the day he'd bidden her farewell, and decided he had waited long enough.

"I have come to request permission to marry your daughter, Lady Catherine," he said resolutely.

The duke finally deigned to look up. "I am most displeased that my instructions regarding Catherine's stay in Cumberland have been so thoroughly ignored. I suppose I should have known Catherine would find a way to flout me." He eyed Philip contemptuously. "Do you really suppose her to be serious in wishing to marry you?"

"Yes, I do."

"Fool! She does not wish to marry you; she is merely using you to coerce me into allowing her to resume her place in society."

"Catherine would not use anyone so."

"How little you know her! Catherine, marry a countrified yokel? She would die first." The duke laughed. It was not a pleasant sound. "Indeed, I am almost tempted to let her marry you. That would teach her not to defy me!"

Philip choked down his indignation, reminding himself that planting his future father-in-law a facer would not advance his suit. "Then do you give your permission?" he asked.

"Not so fast!" said the duke. "You are nothing like my notion of an eligible suitor."

Philip remembered what Catherine had told him about the duke's plan to marry her to the Marquess of Hornsby, and repressed an impulse to violently denounce the duke's notion of an eligible suitor.

"I understand that you had a marquess in mind for her, but I trust you will allow me to prove to you that I can make Lady Catherine a good husband."

"Lord Hornsby has already taken a wife. Unfortunately, he found himself unwilling to wait for Catherine," said the duke, a look of annoyance passing over his face. "With the result that I now find myself obliged to actually consider the suit of a nobody like yourself."

"I hope you will do so," Philip said, telling himself to ignore His Grace's thoroughly *un*gracious manner. He and Catherine didn't need the duke's blessing, just his approval.

"Very well. Tell me about yourself."

Once again, Philip mastered his annoyance, reminding himself it was for Catherine's sake. He provided the duke with a brief history of his family, and showed him a summary of his assets and recent figures on the income from his estate and the family's other investments. The duke seemed barely to listen, and he leafed through Philip's carefully prepared papers with a negligent hand.

"Enough," he grunted, even before Philip had completed his disclosures. "I am convinced you will be able to support my daughter. Whether she will be happy living on such an income is not my concern."

Philip felt his spirits rise, despite the duke's insulting tone. "So we have your permission to marry?" he asked.

The duke's little eyes glinted. "I have not said that. Come back again—let us say, the day after tomorrow, and we will discuss the matter further."

Philip bit back a rude reply. It seemed the duke wished to toy with him, and with Catherine, before actually making a decision. Philip had thought Catherine was exaggerating when she'd described her father, but now he knew better. He was appalled by the duke's meanness of spirit. His heart ached at the thought that Catherine had had to grow up under the control of such a father, and he vowed then and there to do anything he could to prevent her from falling into His Grace's clutches again. He'd even elope with her if he had to, although he hoped it would not come to that.

However, there was nothing more he could do today.

"Thank you, Your Grace," he said, though the words stuck in his throat, then he bowed and left the room.

It was with profound relief that he mounted the

hack Jane's husband had lent him, and returned to the snug rectory where his sister and her family awaited him. The rest of that day, he tried to conceal his frustration with the duke and enjoy the company of Jane, Robert, and their new baby son.

In the afternoon of the following day, he joined his sister and his small nephew in the garden. As he bounced the baby in his lap, Philip's thoughts turned toward Catherine, and what sort of children they might have. Before he and Felix had played for long, they all heard the clatter of hooves along the lane.

Philip wondered who would be driving at such a pace down the narrow lane. Looking over the wall, he saw Catherine's father pull up in a curricle drawn by a team of glossy chestnuts. The duke wore a many-caped driving coat, and his face was ruddy with some strong emotion.

"Come here!" he shouted, looking at Philip.

Disquieted by the urgency in His Grace's voice, Philip handed Felix to Jane and hurried over to the wall.

"Is something amiss, Your Grace?"

"Do you think I would be here if all were well? No. I have received some damnable news."

"Is it Lady Catherine? Is she well?" Philip asked, heart pounding.

"Lord Staverton has sent me a message from Penrith, to inform me that he and his wife had the misfortune to encounter Lord Verwood there."

Philip had not heard the name before; he looked up, wondering why the duke pronounced it with such loathing.

"So she never mentioned him to you? No, she would not have, I suppose! Verwood is the scoundrel

Catherine planned to elope with a few months ago. No doubt he is searching for her so they can try it again. We have both been duped. Catherine probably sent you here as a ruse to distract both of us from her true plan."

"You are wrong," he replied, appalled that the duke could make such accusations against his own daughter.

"You are a fool not to believe it," said His Grace. "In any case, Verwood is capable of any infamy. It is widely rumored—and I believe it to be true—that he once seduced and abandoned a lady of gentle birth. However, since he had the effrontery to ask me for Lady Catherine's hand, I suppose he is in earnest this time."

Philip felt an urgent fear clutch his heart at the duke's words. "You do not think he would abduct her and take her to Gretna Green?"

"That is exactly what I think," replied His Grace.

"Gretna Green!" he exclaimed. "That is only some forty miles from Lynthwaite!"

"Don't you think I know that? That is why it is imperative we reach Lady Catherine before Verwood does. Yes, *we*. I have decided you must come along. Catherine may have need of a husband before this is over, and I won't have Verwood if I can help it! You will pack your things and be ready to leave with me in ten minutes' time. My carriage is faster than anything you could have driven here. Luckily there will be a full moon tonight; if we don't stop we can reach Lynthwaite by morning. Now hurry!"

Thirteen

Catherine watched a hawk wheel overhead for a moment before returning her gaze to the road winding its way into the valley below her. This evening, as she had done for the past two, she had climbed up Druid's Hill to watch for Philip's return. However, she had not yet seen any carriage at all, let alone the phaeton he had driven to Derbyshire.

The restlessness that had possessed her since he had left was only intensified by the fact that the summer sun lingered late this far north. Thank goodness Aunt Mattie and Aunt Phoebe understood her need to come here at this hour. She needed the solace of this high, windy place, with its lichen-encrusted stones, its short springy turf dotted with heather and furze bushes, blooming in shades of purple and gold. Here she could sit and pray wordless prayers for Philip's success in dealing with her father.

She had almost given up her watch when she finally saw it: a carriage of some sort, wending its way into the valley. In the distance, she could just make out a single driver, and two horses. It was enough. It must be Philip!

If she hurried, she would be able to greet him. She sprang up and ran across the hilltop toward the foot-path leading down through the woods to the road. As fast as she could, she ran down the sloping path, occasionally dislodging small stones that rolled treacherously underfoot. Several times she nearly fell, but she didn't care. Philip was back, and she could not wait another instant to know how he had fared.

At last she broke free of the trees, and ran across the pasture that separated the woods from the road. A bend in the road, combined with a slight rise in the valley floor, prevented her from seeing the oncoming carriage, but she was certain she'd reached the road in time. She sat down upon the stile, feeling warm and breathless, and full of nervous anticipation.

Finally she heard the sound of hooves and carriage wheels. A phaeton came round the bend; then she saw with shock and disappointment that it was not Philip driving those matched bays toward her. It was Verwood!

An instant later he drew up abreast of the stile. His dark eyes flashed, and his teeth gleamed against his tanned face as he greeted her.

"My dear Lady Catherine," he drawled. "I was searching for you, but never dreamed I would be so lucky as to find you waiting for me by the road. Looking so very fetching, too!"

Catherine knew her hair was disheveled and her cheeks rosy from her run. Clearly, Verwood did not mind, but she was in no mood for his gallantry.

"I was not waiting for you," she said tartly. "What are you doing here?"

"Softly, darling! Why are you so ungrateful? I have been searching for you high and low. If I had not received word from your friend Miss Hutton, informing me that she had received a letter from you posted from Penrith, I might still be looking. As it is, I had to travel from Penrith to Keswick before I had positive news of your whereabouts."

"But why have you come?"

"Is it not obvious? I am still in need of a wife, and since there is no one who could possibly suit me so well, I have come to rescue you from your exile."

She took a deep breath in an attempt to calm herself. It was not fair to blame Verwood; only a few months ago she would have welcomed him. But now she wanted him gone. If they were seen together, there might be gossip. After all Philip had endured watching her with Captain Maldon and Lord Staverton, she was not going to give him any further cause to doubt her faithfulness.

"I thank you, but I do not need to be rescued," she said with all the dignity she could muster.

"I don't understand," he said. "Do you not wish to escape this godforsaken place?"

She shook her head, unsure whether she should tell him about Philip or not. At one time she had thought she could trust Verwood, but now she realized how little she truly knew about him. She did not know what mischief he might cause.

"Catherine, come and ride with me for a while. We must talk, but I cannot leave my horses standing in the road like this."

"You had better just turn around and return the way you came. It is late; I must go home."

"So cruel! I come all this way, and all you can do is send me away?" He rolled his eyes theatrically.

"I am sorry, but trust me, it is for the best."

"How can I believe that? I do not know what they have done to break your spirit, *ma belle,* but I intend to stay until I find out. You see, I know you are living at Larkspur Cottage, with your great-aunts. The Miss Arndales, I believe. If you do not get up into the carriage with me now, I have only to go there and call upon all of you."

Catherine was torn. She felt reluctant to go with him, but she did not dare let him penetrate further into the valley, toward the village. There would be no way of stilling the gossip then.

"Very well," she said. "Upon condition that you turn around and drive in the direction you came. You can set me down back by the bridge. I shall walk home from there."

She watched him expertly turn his phaeton around in the narrow road, then accepted his hand up into it. She looked around as she sat down. Fortunately, there was no one about to see them.

"So, my lady, you must explain to me just why you don't wish to be rescued anymore. Do not tell me someone has supplanted me in your affections!"

She remained silent. After a pause he continued, "I see that someone has. Some dreadfully dull gentleman farmer, I imagine."

"He is not dull!"

"So I was right. Where is this paragon of rustic charm?"

"At Whitgrave."

"My, my! How appallingly conventional! But how sad it makes me: the spirited Lady Catherine, buried year round with a red-faced squire!"

"He is not a red-faced squire!"

"My apologies," he said, dropping his teasing tone. "Seriously, you do understand that this is precisely what your father had planned for you when he wished you to marry Hornsby?"

She paused to consider. She had always assumed her father would refuse his suit; she had not considered that the duke might think the remoteness of Philip's home an advantage.

"I hope you are right!"

Verwood looked surprised at her vehement answer.

"Do you truly believe this farmer of yours will make you happy?"

She nodded.

"What of all our plans? I thought you wished to travel, to see the world?"

"Philip and I have talked of travel. Perhaps just into Scotland at first, but then, when the children are older—"

"Children?" he interrupted, raising his eyebrows. "Good God, is he a widower with a parcel of brats he expects you to raise?"

"No," she said stiffly. "He does have brothers and sisters for whom he is responsible."

"And you are going to try to be a mother to them? What a wretched thought! I don't know who I pity more."

She was silent. She could not pretend she had any qualities to recommend her for such a role, only good intentions.

"Have you thought about whether you will be able to make *him* happy?"

Verwood's question smote her like an unexpected blow. Philip loved her; she knew that beyond doubt. But it was precisely that love that made him vulnerable. He had already had much to bear: her evasions, her encouragement of Captain Maldon, that whole disastrous incident with Staverton. Making people happy had never been her strong suit.

"I shall try," she said aloud.

"Do you think you will succeed?" he asked softly. "Catherine *ma belle,* how long do you really think you can live amongst these people and pretend to be one of them? How long do you think you can deny what you are?"

He gazed at her, and she saw the wicked lights in his dark eyes. He desired her, and she did not trust the intent she saw in his expression.

"Do not touch me," she said.

"Very well, I won't," he replied, in a velvet tone. "Much as I would enjoy it, I do not need to touch you. Just sitting beside you—this subtle stroking of limb against limb as the carriage moves—is enough for now. Can you deny that you feel it, too, sweet Catherine?"

Damn him! she thought, looking away. He had succeeded in making her conscious of his manly appeal. It was nothing so strong as what she felt sitting beside Philip, and yet she felt . . . something. She could not deny it.

"No, I cannot," she said in a low voice. "I may have wanton tendencies, but I shall make certain Philip never finds out!"

"It is impossible to deny one's own nature for too long," he said, in an earnest tone that contrasted strangely with his earlier mockery. "To try to do so is to risk heartache and disillusionment for everyone."

She turned away, unwilling to hear what he said, but unable to answer either. In her mind, she could see again the pain in Philip's eyes the night of the assembly in Keswick.

"Catherine, you are like a wolf among sheep here.

I, on the other hand, am another wolf. You cannot harm me."

She tried not to listen, to not let his words poison her hopes.

"Are you saying that I would not be faithful to Philip?" she demanded.

"Oh, I am sure you have every intention of being faithful," he said. "I am just saying it is not in your nature—or your blood—to do so."

"What are you saying? I know my father has had mistresses. Many men do so; it does not mean *I* cannot be faithful."

"It is not the duke of whom I speak."

She shuddered, feeling as if a cold hand had taken hold of her heart. Verwood took the reins in one hand and slid his other arm around her waist. "I am sorry to have to tell you this, darling," he said. "But you really should know."

"No!" she cried, shaking his arm off. "I do not believe you. My mother was never unfaithful to my father."

"Perhaps not," he said. "Have you never wondered why you bear so little resemblance to the duke?"

"I am said to resemble my mother," she retorted. "But she had brown eyes, and mine are blue, like His Grace's. Like my father's!" she corrected herself fiercely.

"Come, Catherine. Watery orbs like *his* would never be likened to delphiniums, or a midnight sky. No, you owe your delightful eyes to a quite different man."

The cold hand around her heart began to squeeze.

"How do you know?" she demanded.

"My father told me the story. He knew many such secrets; you could say it was part of his livelihood to do so. For years, he paid his gambling debts with various sums collected in repayment for his silence," Verwood said with a curled lip. "In this case, he was actually visiting at Whitgrave when he was so fortunate as to intercept a letter from your mother to a certain tall and blue-eyed musician hired to entertain the party at the castle. Apparently music was not his only talent, for later the duchess wrote to inform him she was carrying *his* child."

Catherine longed to shut the words out, but she could not. Verwood's story explained so many things. Her appearance, her musical bent. The fact that her father—how *His Grace* had always treated her as an outsider. No doubt his pride had forced him to accept her as his own, but that would only have made him despise her more. She should have suspected; perhaps she had always known, and had hidden it from herself.

"What happened to my father?"

Verwood looked grave. "He set sail for America before you were born. The ship sank, I'm afraid."

"Why have I never heard this before?"

"His Grace took care to hush the matter up. To be cuckolded within a year of marrying, with one he considered a mere hired servant, and before he'd even been presented with an heir! He could not allow such a tale to circulate. He paid my father all he was asked, and no doubt did the same for any servants who suspected. There was still a little gossip, perhaps, but most of the fools in the *haut ton* were too afraid of offending a duke to allow it to go any further. I still have the original letter, back home at Tregaron; you may burn it if you like. Of course, some of the older generation still remember. No doubt that is why Staverton withdrew his suit last Season."

She began to shudder as she finally accepted the truth. Verwood put his arm around her again, and this time she was too overset to protest.

"Don't cry, darling. I haven't the slightest wish to make you miserable, only to prove to you that you were not made for a life of respectable domesticity. Unlike that fool Staverton, I am not the least bit shocked or troubled by your birth. That is precisely why you should marry me."

She hurt too much to even cry. She knew highborn ladies sometimes presented their husbands with children who were not their own. However, they were usually fathered by other peers; far different to be the daughter of a duchess and a hired musician! She could not drag Philip or his family into such shame and degradation. Even if the gossip were never revived, she would always have to live with the knowledge of the past, and fear of what it might mean for the future.

"Marry me, Catherine. You know your respectable suitor will never understand you as I can," Verwood whispered in her ear.

Still she struggled with her decision. Could she, knowing what she knew, go back to Philip? She would never hide such a secret from him, but what would he do if she told him everything?

He would stand by her, of that she was certain. He was too honorable to do otherwise, and no doubt he still felt himself indebted to her for saving Lizzie's life. But his love for her would be shaken, perhaps destroyed forever. Their marriage would be poisoned by doubt and anxiety, and would end in heartache for both of them, sooner or later.

"Tell me you will marry me, Catherine," Verwood

repeated softly. "You know it is the wisest, most merciful thing to do. For your own sake, and for his."

She looked up at him. Verwood's expression was earnest and sincere. He meant what he was saying, and she could not deny the truth of what he said. It would be cruel and selfish to drag Philip into the sordid mess that was her life.

But what would she do then? She could not return to Lynthwaite; it would be unbearable for both her and Philip. Nor could she bear the thought of returning to the duke's control. He might take her back to Whitgrave, but it was not her home, and never had been. She had no home, nor did she have the independent means to make one for herself.

The bleakness of despair washed over her.

"It seems I have no choice," she said. "I will marry you."

"Very good," he said, seeming unmoved by her desolate acceptance of his proposal. "You may not think so now, but I assure you, you *will* be happier this way."

She looked about her, suddenly aware that she had lost all sense of their whereabouts. Now she saw, with a sense of fatality, that they had nearly reached the main road between Keswick and Penrith. She remembered driving up this way with Philip just over a week ago. She nearly broke into tears at the memory. She had been so happy then!

Verwood drove on in silence for the next few miles. In Troutbeck, they changed horses and instead of heading toward Penrith to join the main north road, as Catherine had expected, Verwood chose a less well-traveled road leading roughly northward.

"Yes, I am taking the less obvious route," he said,

as if reading her thoughts. "Unfortunately, I had a rather unpleasant encounter with Staverton and his new wife in Penrith, and I fear that while I was driving to Keswick and back, they may have sent word to your father. It seems prudent to avoid the main road, in the event that we are being pursued. But do not fret; there will be a full moon and we should reach Scotland tonight." Instantly Catherine thought of Philip.

It would be just like Staverton and Lydia to send word to the duke about Verwood. Would Philip hear of it? Would he believe she was faithless enough to willingly run off with Verwood? Then she realized it didn't matter. Philip would learn soon enough that she had done just that. With a sharp pang, she realized just how bitter a blow she was inflicting on his loyal, loving heart. Perhaps it was best he didn't know that she did it to spare him a lifetime of pain. Perhaps it would speed his recovery if he thought her faithless and undeserving of his love.

As they continued on the rough road, she realized Philip was not the only one she was wounding. Her aunts would be terribly worried about her disappearance. She would have to send word as soon as possible to reassure them of her safety, though it would be too much to hope for their forgiveness.

It seemed she was doomed to bring grief to everyone she cared for. Thank goodness she and Philip had not told the children what his errand was in Derbyshire, to spare them the disappointment if he was not successful. However, when she realized she would probably never see them again, her chest ached with suppressed sobs. She had heard of people dying from internal bleeding and wondered if this was how it felt.

Perhaps ten more weary miles passed, and they

changed horses again at Hesket Newmarket. Mercifully, Verwood did not try to converse with her. Eventually she would have to bestir herself to find out what he planned for them, but for now all she could bear was to sit beside him with her bleak thoughts.

A sudden bump as the phaeton passed over a stone protruding from the road aroused Catherine from her abstraction. She noticed now that the road he had chosen was even rougher than before. The setting sun's slanting rays threw strange, deep shadows across the road, no doubt making it more difficult for Verwood to avoid obstructions. She could see he was not pleased with their slow progress.

About ten minutes later, they came to grief. Catherine felt another bump, then a jarring lurch which nearly threw her clear of the phaeton. Verwood instantly flung an arm around her, then worked to calm the horses. A rather placid pair, they quickly settled in response to Verwood's soothing voice. The phaeton stood at a drunken angle, and Catherine saw one of the front wheels lying a short distance away. Verwood handed her the reins, and got down out of the phaeton to inspect the damage and check the horses. She could hear him swearing softly as he did so. When he returned to her, however, his expression was resolutely cheerful.

"I am sorry, *ma belle*. We will not be able to go any further this evening. However, we are in luck, for I believe there is a village up ahead. If you will help me, we can lead the horses there and find a place to spend the night. We should be able to find a wheelwright and resume our journey tomorrow."

She nodded, feeling curiously numb and uncaring. He helped her down from the carriage, and together they freed the horses from the phaeton. She held them while he pulled the carriage off to the side of the road.

Fortunately, neither of the horses appeared to have taken any harm from the accident. She took one, and Verwood took the other, and they left the rough road to walk down an even rougher lane, signposted toward Ullsbeck, toward where they could see lights and the smoke of chimneys rising straight in the still evening air.

"Good! There is an inn," said Verwood as they neared the village. Catherine saw a small but respectable-looking inn. A few minutes later, they passed under the sign of the Fox and Grouse and into the stable yard.

Verwood called out as they approached, and a surprised-looking ostler came out in response. The ostler took away the horses, and Catherine followed Verwood into the inn. They entered the taproom, where they were met by the inn-keeper and his wife. A sudden shock penetrated Catherine's numbness when Verwood introduced them as Mr. and Mrs. Bates, on their way to holiday in Scotland, and asked for the best bedchamber. It seemed he intended to antici-pate their vows.

Too soon, an inner voice cried. She would have to share a bed with Verwood eventually, but did it have to be tonight?

However, she remained silent, not wishing to make the innkeepers any more suspicious than they already looked. She suspected she and Verwood were not the first eloping couple to stay here, though perhaps the least in love.

"And a small supper in a private parlor, if you have one," Verwood concluded with one of his charming smiles. "Just some cold meat and cheese will do."

The innkeepers, no doubt impressed by his manner

and the elegance of his attire, seemed all eagerness to serve him. They promised Verwood their single private parlor, and summoned a maid to conduct Catherine to the best bedchamber.

While Verwood requested that someone be sent to fetch his portmanteau and discussed arrangements for a wheelwright to repair the phaeton, Catherine went up to the bedchamber, where she perfunctorily removed her bonnet, rearranged her hair, and washed her face and hands, all the while feeling a growing sense of wrongness. She reminded herself that she had left Lynthwaite to spare Philip further grief, but a defiant inner voice continued to berate her for her faithlessness.

She came back to the taproom, which was empty save for a single traveler, a pleasant-faced young man who stared at her for a moment, then blushed and apologized incoherently in a Scottish brogue, looking as if he would like to dive down into his tankard. She nodded absently at the young Scotsman, then crossed the room and entered the private parlor, where Verwood awaited her.

"Ah, there you are, my lovely Catherine!" he said. "Another moment and I might have been so rude as to start without you. I have not eaten since noon today, and I must confess I am famished!"

He pulled out a chair for her at the small table, which had been laid with two settings, a cold roast, cheese, bannocks, and a decanter of wine.

"Let me carve you some of this beef," he said.

"Thank you, but no, I am not hungry," she replied.

She saw he looked worried, and decided it would do neither of them any good if she starved herself.

"One of those bannocks, perhaps," she said, taking one with an attempt at a smile.

"Let me pour you some wine. This is quite a tolerable claret for such an out-of-the-way place," he said, pouring some into a glass for her. She noticed he had already drained a glass.

The awareness of what was to come lay like a heavy cloud on the horizon. She struggled to eat, though the bread tasted like ashes in her mouth. The wine warmed her just a little, but it could have been seawater for as much as she enjoyed it.

"Where shall we go when we are married?" she asked.

"Anywhere you wish, darling. We could go to Tregaron. It's in Cornwall, you know. A rather wild sort of place, but if you like, we can go there."

She noticed a hesitation in his manner, and concluded the thought of his home gave him little pleasure.

"I should like to see it someday," she said politely. "But there is no hurry."

"We might go to the Continent," he continued. "Or if you like, we could stay in Scotland, perhaps tour the Highlands."

"No, please, not Scotland!" she cried, remembering how Philip had talked to her of going there together. Realizing how distraught she sounded, she added in a calmer voice, "I should prefer to see France and Italy, please."

"It will be my pleasure to show them to you." He took a leisurely sip of his wine.

She looked down at the ruby dregs in her own glass. A few months ago she had dreamt of this: traveling the world with a rake experienced in all its ways. Now she could not feel more indifferent to the prospect.

"More wine?" Without waiting for her reply, Verwood refilled both their glasses.

Absently, Catherine drained her glass, and found it did nothing to lighten her despondency. She looked up and saw Verwood watching her with a look of concern.

"I wish you would not look so stricken, *ma belle,*" he said lightly. "I promise you I will be no ogre of a husband."

"No, I do not think that. It is only . . ."

The maid reentered to clear the dishes, and Catherine went to stand by the window. She had to master this aching depression; she could not let Verwood know how she had hoped for a future with Philip. Verwood was cynical; he would laugh.

The maid left them, and Verwood came to stand beside Catherine. He snaked an arm around her waist, and pulled her toward him. His suave, practiced hold felt wrong. It was nothing like Philip's heartfelt embrace.

Instinctively, she pushed him away. "I am sorry. I cannot. It is too soon."

He made no attempt to reclaim her, but stood watching her with a question in his eyes. "My dear, surely you are not worrying about conventions at a time like this? We are going to be married tomorrow."

No doubt he meant to reassure her, but his words struck her ears like a death knell. She put her hands up to cover her face, so he would not see her sorrow.

"However, there is no need to rush things," he said softly. His arms came around her again, and he stroked her back in a manner clearly meant to soothe. Unresisting, she let him lead her to a sofa along one wall of the room and seat her at one end of it. He sat down beside her and again put his arms around her. This time, Catherine willed herself to accept his embrace. As he had said, they were going to be married tomorrow. She had to learn to accept his attentions.

"Catherine, I will do nothing you do not wish," he said. "But you must at least let me show you how pleasant our life together will be."

He kissed her, a mere brush of the lips, yet somehow it was practiced and sensual. She tasted the claret on his lips. He tasted strange. Wrong.

"Don't resist me, Catherine," said Verwood, his voice lowered. "This is not evil, though there are those who will tell you so. Think of it as a pleasure, the most delightful pleasure that a man and a woman can share, just like a bottle of fine wine."

She closed her eyes and forced herself to remain still as he kissed her again, this time more deeply, more thoroughly, with a skill he had practiced on no doubt hundreds of women. She was aware of his breath, his lips, his arm around her, and yet she felt nothing. Nothing except a cold, dull ache where her heart had been.

He redoubled his efforts. Finally, with an odd sense of detachment, she began to feel her body respond to his attentions. Perhaps if she could ignore her guilt, the sensation would grow, and she could drown in pleasure like a drunkard, forgetting her pain as the drunkard forgot his pain by the sixth bottle.

Prompted perhaps by her lack of response, Verwood released her lips and lowered his head to kiss her on the shoulder, then on the neck, then on the sensitive place under her ear.

She tensed.

Philip had kissed her just there, the night of the assembly at Keswick. But it had been nothing like Verwood's expert lovemaking; Philip's kisses had been wild and tender, loving and passionate, and they had aroused her in a way that Verwood never could. She hadn't felt dull and submissive; she had been rapturous, eager to return Philip's ardor with a matching passion of her own.

Perhaps this was not evil in itself; but it was wrong, in comparison with what could be.

"No," she said, and twisted out of Verwood's arms.

"What? What is amiss?" he asked huskily, and tried to pull her toward him again.

"No, I cannot do this," she said, jumping up from the sofa.

"Very well, my darling, if you wish to wait—"

"No, I mean I cannot marry you!"

He arose from the sofa and scowled as he faced her. "What? You will not marry me?" he asked, in a sharpened voice.

She shook her head.

"I have searched for you the length and breadth of the country, taken you from that miserable cottage in that godforsaken valley, and now you will not marry me? Why? Do you think to return to your rustic suitor?"

"I must."

"Will you tell him about your father? What do you think he will say?"

"I don't know," she said, pacing restlessly about the room. "I think he won't care! Why did I ever listen to you? He told me to believe in our love, and I failed him!"

"Do you think he will forgive you this escapade? Or do you think to keep it a secret?"

"I must tell him the truth. I don't know if he will forgive me, but I must try. I don't deserve him, but I do love him. I think I could make him happy!"

Verwood stared at her for a moment. "Catherine, you could drive a saint mad!" he said, but his voice was calmer now. "I thought you were deluding yourself with your plans to live in pastoral seclusion with this farmer of yours, but I suppose you must really be in love. That, or I have quite lost my touch. I do not think I have ever had to work quite so hard to console a lady."

Catherine was relieved to hear a humorous note creep into his voice. "Will you take me home, please?" she asked.

"Very well, I will take you back to Lynthwaite tomorrow, as soon as the phaeton has been repaired. Hopefully your aunts will not have raised too great a hue and cry over your absence."

She stopped her pacing. She had forgotten all about the phaeton. "Tomorrow morning! There must be some other carriage we could hire. It is a moonlit night. If we leave now, we can reach the valley before dawn and I could pretend I lost my way in the hills."

"I am sorry," he said. "There is no other carriage; the only one that is kept here is in Carlisle tonight."

"Can we ride then?"

He shook his head. "The only riding horse in the stables is that young Scotsman's cob, and the poor beast has already done better than twenty miles today."

"Is there nothing else we can do? I must get back!"

"I know we are in a fix," he said. "But rushing off

into the night won't solve it. I will take you home to your aunts tomorrow. We can think of some tale to tell them, perhaps, and remember, no one here knows our true names."

She was silent. She could see it was futile to argue any further, though she could not accept Verwood's plan. Perhaps she could still avoid an open scandal; perhaps if she returned before morning, Philip would believe her account of what had happened, and forgive her.

She had to think of something.

"We should get some rest," said Verwood. "It would look very strange if I requested another room, so I suppose I must sleep on the floor tonight. If anyone knew, how my reputation would suffer!"

He chuckled, but Catherine was barely aware of it.

"You can trust me, Catherine," he said more earnestly. "I have never forced myself on an unwilling lady, and I will not do so now."

"I believe you," she said, busily thinking of her next course of action.

"I see you do," he said, with a rueful smile. "Very well. I suggest you go up to the bedchamber now and prepare yourself. There is a rather delectable nightdress in the portmanteau; I had hoped to enjoy the sight of you wearing it, but alas! I suppose one must endure some disappointments in life. I shall come up in about fifteen minutes. I expect by that time all feminine charms will be safely hidden under the bedcovers!"

She smiled, thanked him, and left the room. The taproom was empty now, thank goodness. Instead of heading up the stairs to the bedchamber, she hurried outside and made her way quickly and quietly to the stables.

In the moonlight, she saw the two horses Verwood had driven, hanging their heads out of adjacent stalls. Beyond them, the Scotsman's cob stood calmly nibbling at some hay. The poor beast did look tired; she would have to try riding one of the carriage horses. Now if only she could find a saddle and bridle. She tried the door of the harness room, but unfortunately it was locked.

She paused, temporarily at a loss. Verwood would discover her absence if she delayed much longer. Resolutely, she led one of the carriage horses out of his stall on his halter. There was a mounting block just outside the stable. She led the horse up to it, and paused, gathering her courage. Ages ago, she had played truant riding her pony astride and bareback. She could do it again.

She swung herself on, cursing the encumbrance of her skirts.

"Who's there?"

It sounded like the ostler. She had to hurry!

She rode out of the stable yard and down the lane, guiding the beast with her legs. He was unwilling at first, balking at leaving his mate and his comfortable stable, but after she slapped him on the rump, he reluctantly broke into a trot. She took care to sit up, and not grip too tightly with her knees, despite the feeling that she might slip off the horse at any moment.

They had nearly rejoined the main road when she heard voices in the distance. The ostler and Verwood, she thought.

"Stop! Thief!"

"Catherine! Come back! This is insane."

She tried to urge the horse to greater speed, but he flattened his ears and refused to do more than trot. She slapped him again on the hindquarters. This time, he gave a small, protesting buck, and she nearly lost her already precarious seat as he finally broke into a canter.

Now she heard hoofbeats behind her. Verwood was pursuing her, no doubt, but perhaps she still had enough of a start on him. She held on to the horse's mane, trying to maintain her seat, and realized the futility of her actions. Verwood was the most accomplished of riders; she had no chance of outracing him, particularly under these conditions.

Still, she could not bear to give up.

Her horse slowed, probably sensing his mate coming up behind him. She tried once more to send him forward, but this time, he bucked in earnest. She felt a momentary sensation, oddly peaceful, of flying up through the cool night air, then a sharp, jagged pain that shot through her ankle as she landed on the stony surface of the road. She crumpled, and went down.

For an instant, all was pain, and turmoil, and stamping hooves. Then her horse veered around and headed back toward Verwood and the other horse. Shortly, Verwood rode up, the horse she had just ridden trailing behind.

Verwood dismounted and ran toward her.

"Catherine, you madwoman! Are you hurt?"

"I think I have sprained my ankle," she said, sitting up.

"No more than you deserve, for trying something so stupid. You could have been killed! Does anything else hurt?"

She shook her head. Now, finally the tears came, as

pain and despair washed over her. She had failed once again.

"Hush, darling," said Verwood, in a softened voice. "I suppose I should have known not to trust you to go to bed meekly as you were bid!"

He helped her to stand, but when she tried to take a step, she found she could not. Verwood swept her up in his arms, carried her to the horse he had ridden, and put her up on its back. Her tears continued to flow as he led the two horses back toward the inn again.

She heard Verwood curse under his breath as they approached the inn once more. Dimly, she was aware of a crowd of people all in the stable yard, excitedly shouting about horse thieves. As they entered the yard, the shouting subsided, and she looked dazedly at the faces of the ostler, the innkeeper, the innkeeper's wife, the chambermaid and the young Scotsman, all staring back at them in surprise.

Verwood squared his shoulders as he faced them, and she tried to wipe her tears.

"Please help me get my wife back into the inn," he said, taking her off the horse. "She had a premonition that our child had fallen ill, and being of an excitable disposition, she did not wish to wait until tomorrow to return to him."

The assembled crowd did not look convinced.

"I am sorry to have created such a stir," she said, summoning up the last of her energy in an attempt to smile.

Everyone looked a little reassured. The ostler took the horses away, while everyone else followed Verwood as he carried Catherine into the inn and up the stairs to their bedchamber.

Through her misery, she was dimly aware of Verwood laying her down on the bed, removing her half boots, of the landlady examining her ankle and applying a cold compress to it, of Verwood pressing her to drink a glass of wine. As she swallowed it, she wondered at the odd, sweet taste.

"There's laudanum in it, my dear. It will help you sleep," she heard him say.

Gradually, a numbness stole over her. The pain in her ankle began to recede, but the ache in her heart remained. *Forgive me, Philip, I tried,* she thought before sliding into a welcome oblivion.

Fourteen

Dawn was breaking as Philip drove the duke's curricle up to lane toward Larkspur Cottage, His Grace beside him. He and the duke had driven all night, taking turns driving after each change of horses. They'd made good time, but still he prayed that they were not too late.

During the drive, Catherine's father had recounted enough of Lord Verwood's history to make Philip's blood run cold at the thought that Catherine might have fallen into the rake's clutches. It was also easy to see that some past feud lay between the duke and the notorious baron. He hoped Catherine was not already a victim of their enmity.

A few more minutes and the cottage was in sight. Once again Philip prayed. *Let her be here. Let them all still be asleep,* he silently pleaded as he halted the horses in front of the cottage.

To his dismay, the door flew open and both of Catherine's aunts peered out eagerly. They were fully dressed, and their faces were pale and drawn, as if they'd been up the entire night. For an instant they stared up at Philip and the duke, and he could see the anxious hope in their eyes fade to disappointment.

Then the duke spoke.

"Where is Lady Catherine?" he asked abruptly.

Miss Matilda came forward to answer. "Your Grace, she went out walking last evening and never returned. We fear she may be lost or hurt in the hills somewhere."

"Damn her! Damn her!" the duke exploded. "She is not lost; she has run off with that scoundrel Verwood. To think I trusted all of you to keep watch over her! What a stupid, incompetent pack of—"

"Quiet!" Philip shouted. The duke glared at him, but ceased his tirade. Philip turned to Miss Matilda. "When did you last see Catherine?"

"She went out for a walk last evening, after supper," said Miss Matilda. "Every night since you left she has gone up the hill to look for your return. Your Grace, I could swear she has not thought of Lord Verwood in months!"

"What has been done to find her? Has anyone seen anything?" asked Philip.

"Jemima and Ned have been looking for her all night, and some of the other valley folk have joined them in the search. Ned is due to return in another half an hour. We were hoping he would bring better news."

"Fools!" said the duke. "They may already be married. Damn him! Damn her!"

"He may have abducted her," said Philip, finally accepting the grim possibility. "But she would not marry him. He could not force her to do so. Unless . . ." He broke off, assailed by an even more agonizing suspicion.

"Unless what?" asked Miss Matilda.

"Unless she thinks she is ruined," said Philip, the words wrung out of him. "If they stopped somewhere for the night, and . . ."

"You may be right," said the duke. "Perhaps they are not already married. There is still hope."

Philip stared at the duke. What sort of monster was he to react so calmly to the prospect of his own daughter's ruination?

"I assume you are still willing to marry her?" asked the duke.

"Yes, of course I am!"

"Good! Then let us continue this damned chase. Miss Arndale, you are to set it about that you have found Catherine, that she was injured out walking on the hills and is too unwell to see anyone. If we reach her in time, we will bring her back here in a closed carriage so no one will be the wiser."

Miss Matilda agreed. Quickly, Philip drove the curricle into the yard beyond the cottage. He turned it around there, and then drove it back in their earlier direction, forcing himself not to push the horses to too fast a pace. The next change was still miles off; he would have to nurse the horses through until they could be relieved.

After a few anxious miles, they reached Troutbeck. While a new team was being put to the curricle, they made some inquiries and learned that a phaeton driven by a gentleman answering to Verwood's description had passed through there the previous evening. According to their informants, the gentleman had been accompanied by a striking dark-haired lady. No one said anything to indicate the lady was being coerced, which His Grace interpreted to mean that Catherine had planned to marry Verwood all along. Philip refused to believe it, yet he could not help wondering why his resourceful love had not made some attempt to escape her captor.

Being familiar with the region, Philip continued to drive, following the less traveled but more direct northward route Verwood had been seen to take. It was still early morning when they reached Hesket Newmarket, where they procured another change of horses and learned that Verwood and Catherine had stopped there as well.

Philip forced himself to ignore his fears and concentrate on driving as quickly as he could on the increasingly rough road. Either way, he was too late to do anything about what had happened last night. All he could do now was to find Catherine, and help her recover from whatever ordeal she had suffered.

After about three more agonizing miles, they encountered a solitary horseman, a young man riding southward on a gray cob. He would have passed them with just a tip of the hat, but the duke called out for him to stop.

"We are seeking a pair of runaways," he said. "Have you seen a gentleman and a lady who appear to be on their way to Gretna Green?"

"Aye, there was a couple that stayed last night at the Fox and Grouse," the young Scotsman replied, looking uncomfortable. "They called themselves Mr. and Mrs. Bates and said they were on holiday, but I didna think that was the truth."

"What did they look like?" asked the duke.

"I didna notice the gentleman much, but the lady, sir! Oh the lady! I am a poet, but I canna find the reet words to describe her beauty! A goddess, with hair like a raven's wing and eyes like sapphires. Those eyes—"

"Enough! It is she," said the duke, looking at Philip. "Had they left the inn yet?"

"Nay, there was an accident to their carriage. The

wheelwright is mending it as we speak. I do hope the poor lass will be able to travel, after all that happened last night."

"What happened?" asked Philip.

"Och, she tried to run away. Perhaps 'twas nerves due to the wedding. She stole one of the carriage horses and tried to ride him away on just his halter, but the beast threw her."

"Dear God! Was she badly hurt?"

"Naught worse than a sprained ankle, I ken. The gentleman brought her back weeping fit to break your heart. He made some tale to explain it all, and she agreed. To my thinking, 'twas just some lovers' quarrel and not my place to meddle."

"How far is it, this Fox and Grouse?" asked the duke.

"Half a mile farther, in Ullsbeck."

"Drive on, Woodmere," said the duke impatiently. "We are almost upon them!"

Mechanically, Philip thanked the young poet and drove on. He could barely see, tormented as he was by the mental image of Catherine struggling so desperately to escape from Verwood, only to be brought back to the inn, injured and at the mercy of such a scoundrel.

"I should have listened to her! I should never have gone to Derbyshire!" he burst out, involuntarily.

"Don't complain, Woodmere. Remember all's well that ends well."

"How can you say that?" he asked, looking at His Grace with ever-rising loathing.

"You heard that Scotsman. They have not left that inn yet, and it is only a few miles off. We should be there in plenty of time to stop them from setting off again."

"But what about Catherine? What about your daughter?"

"My concern is to avert a scandal, and I believe we may do that. Are you concerned for her virtue, fool? It is my belief she lost *that* last year."

Philip halted the horses. He gathered the whip and the reins into one hand; he took hold of the duke's throat with the other.

"Do not ever say such things of your daughter again," he said, giving His Grace a small, threatening shake. "Do you hear me?"

The duke's eyes bulged with fear, then he nodded. Philip released him and urged the horses on again, though anger still coursed through him. He was a peaceable man, loath to abuse the natural advantages of his size and strength against the weak and cowardly. He hadn't raised his fists against anyone since boyhood. But he was sorely tempted now, by this abominable peer who treated his daughter with such callous unconcern.

Renewed fear for Catherine routed his anger, and Philip drove on recklessly, once again sending urgent prayers upward for her well-being.

Catherine sat with Verwood in the parlor in which they had supped the night before. She tried to drink some tea and eat some toast, though her stomach churned at the sight and smell of the ham and eggs Verwood·was cheerfully consuming for his breakfast. Her ankle had swollen considerably overnight and she had a tearing headache, the result of having taken too much wine and laudanum last night, and little else. However, all these ills were as nothing compared to the misery in her heart.

"Are you quite certain you feel well enough to travel today?" Verwood asked, looking anxious.

Catherine was not at all surprised by his expression. If she looked even half as wretched as she felt, she must be a sight. But it didn't matter.

"Yes, I can travel," she said. "I cannot bear to stay here one more minute than necessary."

"Shall I tell you the story I have concocted?" he asked, then continued in response to her nod. "You walked too far last night, lost your way, and sprained your ankle coming down the wrong side of one of the hills. I conveniently passed by this morning and found you, and will, in true gentlemanly fashion, return you to Larkspur Cottage. It will seem a trifle suspicious, I know, but it is the best I can devise. Your poor ankle will at least bear it out. What do you think?"

"It will have to do," she replied. "I can think of nothing better."

She sighed. There would certainly be talk, but perhaps Verwood's story would prevent an outright scandal. She would tell her aunts and Philip the truth, of course.

All her actions of the previous day seemed so insane now. She should have resisted Verwood. She should have trusted in Philip, in the power of their attachment. Would he forgive her for not doing so?

Verwood finished his breakfast and drained his tankard of ale. Once more, he looked at her, his dark eyes troubled.

"Catherine, I suggest you lie down on the sofa and keep your foot up, while I go and see how the repairs on the phaeton are progressing. Perhaps I can hurry them along a little."

He helped her up from her chair and put an arm around her so that she could hobble over to the sofa. As she did so, Catherine heard the sound of a carriage entering the yard. She thought nothing of it; the coach from Carlisle was expected soon. She sat down, then turned and swung her legs up onto the sofa. Verwood put a pillow behind her, then knelt down to position another one under her ailing ankle.

"Such a pretty ankle, even swollen and bandaged," he said, with a heavy sigh. "I quite envy your bucolic lover."

Catherine knew Verwood was only trying to cheer her, so she tried to smile at him.

"Don't worry, darling," said Verwood. "All will be well, I promise—"

"Hush!" she said. She thought she heard a familiar, beloved voice amid the sounds from the taproom. But no, it could not be. Philip could not have pursued them here so quickly. She settled back and closed her eyes, grimacing with pain as Verwood settled her foot onto the second cushion. Verwood was just smoothing her skirts around her ankles, when she heard a quick, heavy tread on the threshold.

"Take your hands off her!"

Instantly, she opened her eyes and turned her head. Philip was standing in the doorway, face haggard and unshaven, and murder in his eyes. Behind him stood her father—no, *not* her father. His Grace the Duke of Whitgrave, her mother's cuckolded husband, looking travel-worn and irritated.

For a tense moment, they all stared at each other in shock.

Then Verwood rose unhurriedly from the foot of the sofa.

"Ah, the irate father and the rustic suitor," he drawled, stepping away from the sofa.

Philip crossed the room in three quick strides and sent Verwood crashing to the floor.

Verwood slowly started to rise; blood spurted from his nose, but Catherine saw his hands curl into fists. Philip stood ready to hit Verwood again.

"No, please stop! Both of you!" she cried, pushing herself up onto one elbow.

Philip turned toward her, remorse replacing the anger in his eyes. "I am sorry, love." He looked back at Verwood. "But after all he's done, abducting you and—"

"He did not abduct me," she interrupted.

Philip stared at her, stunned. "You did not go with him willingly, did you?"

Guilt overwhelmed her as she realized that Philip had believed in her all along. He had believed in her and trusted her, and she had betrayed and wounded him in return. Could she make him understand she had done it for his sake?

"Yes, I went with him willingly," she replied, and saw him recoil, as if she had struck him. "But you must let me explain. Verwood told me—"

"Silence!" shouted the duke. "Not one more word, *daughter,* or it will be the worse for all of you!"

She struggled to sit back up, head swimming with the effort. Evidently, the duke was determined not to let Philip know the truth, and he made no idle threats, as she knew from bitter experience. She had no idea how to counter this one.

"And you, Verwood, take yourself off, and consider

yourself fortunate I have taken no further action against you!"

"Very well, Your Grace. I will relieve you all of my quite unnecessary presence," said Verwood, holding a handkerchief to his nose. He looked at Catherine with a wry smile. *"Adieu, ma belle.* May you find much happiness."

He bowed gracefully and sauntered out of the room.

Catherine looked back at Philip. It seemed as if his face had turned to stone, for all the expression it held now, but his eyes betrayed him. In them she could see exactly the blow she had dealt him. How could she even hope for his forgiveness?

"Philip deserves to hear the truth," she said, looking defiantly at the duke.

"You will tell him nothing," said His Grace. "If you do not obey me, Catherine, I shall begin proceedings to charge Woodmere with a breach-of-promise suit that will ruin him and his family forever. Do you wish that on your conscience?"

Her stomach churned with anger, guilt, and revulsion. His Grace certainly had the wealth and influence to make good on his threat, and he was just mean-spirited enough to enjoy trampling a family like the Woodmeres underfoot. And it was she who had brought this evil upon them. She could not allow it.

"We have no time to waste," His Grace continued. "Catherine, you are to come with me now. I have hired a carriage to take us both back to Whitgrave. Woodmere, you can return the curricle when you come for the wedding."

Catherine stared at him, her thoughts in chaos.

"You are going to be married," he said in an exasperated tone. "I have already ordered my man of business to procure a special license. The wedding will take place in exactly one week's time."

She looked back at Philip, appalled by the tortured look in his eyes. Now it was painfully clear that he was being coerced into this. Her lack of faith had destroyed his love for her. She had broken his heart, but if she could help it, she would not ruin his life.

"You cannot force Philip to marry me," she said to the duke, her voice shaking.

The duke turned to Philip. "You are still willing to marry her, are you not?" he demanded.

"I am." Philip's reply was grim, resolute. Clearly his words were not prompted by love, but out of a sense of honor, or perhaps a lingering gratitude for her having saved Lizzie's life.

"You see," said His Grace, "*he* is willing, so why should you object?"

"This is not right!" she cried. "I won't have him trapped this way."

"Is this necessary, your grace?" asked Philip. "She is in pain. Surely if you would just leave us alone for a few minutes—"

"No! I tell you, the time is past for discussion. You will make your choice, Catherine. Will you marry him or will you ruin him?"

She rubbed her throbbing temples for a moment, though she knew she had no real choice. She could not allow the duke to carry out his threat against Philip and his family. She lowered her hands and straightened back up to give her answer.

"I will marry him."

"At last you see reason! Come along, then."

She reached over to a table beside the sofa for her bonnet. Her hands shook annoyingly as she put it on and struggled to tie the strings. She could not bear to look at Philip.

When she had finished putting on her bonnet, she stood up, and swayed for a moment, dizzy with pain and weakness. With an annoyed look, His Grace came forward to help her, but Philip was quicker. To her surprise, he picked her up, clutching her close to his chest. She rested her head against his shoulder and drew a measure of comfort from his familiar scent and the warmth of his arms. Perhaps he still felt some remnants of affection for her. No, more likely it was just his innate kindness.

He carried her out of the parlor, through the taproom, and out to the awaiting carriage. After he had placed her gently on the seat, he bade her a soft farewell. She gathered the resolution to look at him, and was stricken to the core by the infinitely weary, bleak expression on his face.

An instant later, Philip was gone, and the duke had climbed in beside her. Waves of pain and nausea pummeled Catherine as the coach rattled off. They were only a faint echo of the agony she felt within, at having ruined the best chance for happiness she had ever been given.

Fifteen

Catherine would always look back on that journey to Whitgrave Castle as a nightmare. Several times during the first few hours, the carriage had to be stopped so she could be sick by the roadside, while His Grace waited impatiently. They stopped in Lynthwaite to collect her baggage and maintain the pretense that she had not left the valley, but Catherine was given no opportunity to speak to her aunts. Back in the carriage, the rocking motion aggravated the throbbing in her head and her ankle, so that it was a relief of sorts when they finally stopped for the night.

The next morning she awoke feeling somewhat recovered in body, but with a heavy ache in her heart. They reached Whitgrave Castle in the early afternoon, and another sort of nightmare began.

The duchess and Lady Susannah greeted her with palpably false sweetness; the guests at the castle with great curiosity. Catherine knew everyone was secretly gossiping about the suddenness of her wedding, though outwardly they all congratulated her on having such a magnanimous father who would permit her to marry according to her heart.

Catherine ignored the whispering and the compliments alike, content for the present to drift along, passively participating in all the fittings for her bride

clothes and other preparations for the wedding, which
was to be more elaborate than was usual. Catherine
could see the duke and duchess hoped that a sufficient
degree of pomp would cover up any taint of scandal.
For Philip's sake, she cooperated, determined that no
one should think she was lowering herself to marry
him.

Four days later, he arrived in Derbyshire, bringing
his brothers and sisters. Catherine was saddened, but
not surprised, to learn that he had decided to stay with
his sister Jane rather than at the castle.

That evening, a dinner party was held at the castle.
It was the first time she had seen Philip since their
parting in Ullsbeck, and there was little comfort in
their meeting. Unlike most engaged couples, they
were not permitted to be alone together, so their conversation was limited to his inquiries after her ankle,
and hers after his brothers and sisters. Philip was composed, but so grave he almost seemed like a stranger.

Also attending the dinner party were Philip's sister
Jane and her husband, Robert. Both the Lambourns
seemed very good-natured. Their unquestioning kindness made Catherine very uncomfortable; they did not
know how little she deserved it.

Later in the evening, still heavily chaperoned, Philip
told her some of his plans. He intended to bring her
straight home to Woodmere Hall, leaving the children
to enjoy a month's holiday with Jane. His cousin
Dorothea had gone to stay with Sir George and Lady
Maldon at Maldon Park, an arrangement he said which
was likely to become permanent. Miss Matilda and
Miss Phoebe were both in good health, and looked forward to seeing Catherine on her return to Lynthwaite.

Catherine felt the stirrings of hope at hearing what

Philip had planned for them. Surely he would not have arranged for them to be alone for a month if he wished for a marriage in name only, which was her worst fear. At least she would have a chance to explain what had happened. He would probably never love her as freely as he had before, but perhaps he would forgive her enough to make a fresh start. However, she could be sure of nothing, except that there was a painful distance between them now, and a deeply troubled look in his eyes that belied his tranquil demeanor.

The following day, on Catherine's invitation, Philip brought the children to the castle. She set them all to playing bowls on the lawn, and ordered lemonade and cakes to be served afterward. The young Woodmeres enjoyed themselves hugely, their only disappointment being the fact that the moat had long since been drained and planted with grass. Catherine almost felt that if left alone with the children, she and Philip might have regained some of their former ease. However, the duchess hovered over them the entire time.

Another day passed in like manner, and then the day of her wedding dawned. Catherine allowed herself to be dressed in the elegant and expensive finery the duchess had chosen for her, a white satin embroidered with tiny pearls, then to be escorted to the castle's chapel, where the ceremony was to be held. All the duke and duchess's guests, including the Earl of Ibstone and his mother, the dowager countess, were in attendance, besides Philip's family and a few other Harcourts the duke had invited. Catherine knew the unusual size of the party was part of the duke's plan to invest the wedding with greater respectability.

Catherine longed for Juliana and Penelope; their presence would have meant more to her than anything else. There had not been time to invite them, nor would the duke and duchess have made them welcome.

She gazed past the crowd of faces and saw Philip. Her budding hopes withered at the sight of him. His face was set, even a little pale under his tan, and she could see from his very stance what a strain it was for him to behave with dignity while being coerced into an unwanted marriage.

She came to stand beside him, trying not to limp too visibly, and struggling to compose her own expression. Enough tongues were probably wagging that the duke was marrying her off to Philip to avoid scandal; perhaps some were laughing at Philip, calling him the duke's pawn. She could not let them think she was anything but willing, so she did her best to smile and appear the happy bride.

It came time to make their vows, and she almost broke into tears at the sound of Philip's rich voice resounding through the lofty chapel. She could not help thinking he really meant the words he said. When she made her own responses, her voice rang out surprisingly clearly, and she realized just how desperately she wished it were all true.

Soon it was over, and she and Philip were accepting everyone's compliments and congratulations, as they passed from the chapel to the old banqueting hall, where a lavish wedding breakfast awaited them. Catherine sat beside Philip, trying to smile and making a pretense of eating the elaborate dishes the duke's French chef had prepared for the occasion. She noticed Philip did not have his usual hearty appetite, either.

However, the duke and duchess were smiling and

looking quite self-satisfied with all the proceedings. His Grace in particular looked over to her with such a fatuous expression of victory that she felt she could not bear the charade much longer. After receiving what seemed like interminable congratulations, some sincere and some otherwise, she joined her stepmother and stepsister, who bore her off toward her bedchamber, to assist her in changing her dress for the journey back to Cumberland.

On their way out of the banquet hall, the duke stopped them.

"I wish to have a word with Catherine before she leaves," he stated. "In my study, please."

The duchess and Lady Susannah obediently returned to the company, and Catherine followed the duke to his study. Already reeling from the stress of the day, she feared some new blow. However, the duke appeared to be in as mellow a mood as she had ever seen him. No doubt it was relief at having finally gotten rid of her.

He motioned for her to sit down in the chair before his desk, and settled himself in his own chair.

"Well, Catherine, you have gotten what you wished for. You are married to your gentleman farmer. I trust you are happy now."

She was silent. She did not know where this was leading, but she was quite certain it was not her happiness His Grace was concerned with.

"Perhaps you are wondering why I wished to see you."

She said nothing, and His Grace continued calmly.

"I brought you here to warn you that if you should ever mention the unfortunate information that Verwood imparted to you, if there is the slightest hint of news from Cumberland that you are not behaving as a respectable married lady, I still have it in my power to make it all the worse for you and your precious Woodmeres."

A new anger overcame her anxiety. She had been fearful long enough. Even if her marriage failed, at least she had gained her freedom from this unloving, spiteful man. How long had she tried to look up to him as a father? Now she saw him for what he was: a weak bully, and one, moreover, who was terribly insecure of his station, and desperately afraid of being made a fool. No wonder he had gone to such lengths to hide the truth of her parentage! But understanding him did not excuse his actions. He had done his best to ruin her life, and Philip's. It was time to show him he could no longer threaten her or anyone she loved.

"I don't think you will dare," she said. "In fact, if you ever say or do anything more that could hurt Philip or his family, I *will* cause a scandal, one which will make you the laughingstock of the *ton*. I shall let everyone know the truth about my mother and her lover, and I shall enjoy doing it!"

He stared at her, eyes bulging in shock at her threat.

"You would not dare!" he cried, his voice quavering with anger and fear. "You would not bring such shame down on Woodmere and that family of his you appear to have become so fond of!"

"I am going to offer Philip the opportunity to divorce me," she said, trying to keep her voice from shaking at the prospect. "Perhaps we can obtain a Scottish divorce; I have heard that is easy enough. Or perhaps we can have the marriage annulled, since I really had no right to sign the name of Harcourt."

Rage suffused the duke's face with a brilliant red.

As she expected, he was horrified by the thought of the scandal attendant on any divorce proceeding.

"Damn you!" he growled. He rose from his chair and came around his desk, looking as if he might try to throttle her.

Catherine got up quickly from her chair and backed toward the door. "If you take another step toward me, I shall scream for help," she said. "That *will* cause a stir."

His face was nearly purple with anger now, but the threat of a scene gave him pause, as she knew it would.

"You do not really wish for a divorce, do you?" he asked in a querulous voice that showed exactly how much he feared the possible scandal.

"No, I do not," she replied. "However, I shall cooperate if Philip wishes it."

"He won't. The fool is totally besotted with you. Why else would he be willing to marry Verwood's leavings?"

She set little store by the duke's conclusions. His mind was incapable of understanding the most likely reasons why Philip had married her: honor, kindness and gratitude. Perhaps even pity.

"He had no choice in the matter," she said aloud. "Now I shall give him one. If we cannot find a way to be happy together, I shall offer Philip his freedom. I think, Your Grace, it is time you wished me happy."

She gazed at him steadily until he lowered his eyes.

"I wish you happy," he muttered.

"Thank you," she said. "I trust you understand now that if you do anything again to harm me or anyone I love, I shall make you rue the day."

She started to leave the room, but turned around on impulse.

"Do you know, Your Grace, if you had only shown me some kindness, you would have had my most fervent devotion. It is a pity, for both of us, that you could not do so. Now I can only be *glad* I am not your daughter."

As she limped up the stairs to her bedchamber, Catherine felt an unaccustomed sense of victory, tinged with regret for what might have been. Doubts for her future assailed her again as she entered the room and saw Her Grace's dignified dresser waiting there, ready to assist her out of her satin and into the dark blue carriage dress that was laid out in readiness for her coming journey. All too quickly she was dressed, her hair tidied and tucked beneath a matching dark blue bonnet from which a black feather arched elegantly.

She looked at herself in the mirror for a moment before leaving the room. The new ensemble was fashionable and becoming, but she hated it; it was just one more costume furnished by the duke and duchess for their little play. Her face seemed pale, so she pinched her cheeks slightly. For just a few more minutes, she had to maintain the appearance of an eager bride and hide her misgivings for the future. Then, finally, she would have her chance to talk to Philip, and see if something could be salvaged from the wretched shambles she'd made of things.

As her stepmother's dresser made some final adjustments to her toilette, her stepmother and stepsister came into the room.

"La! You are already dressed," said Susannah with a giggle. "I see you are eager to be off with your husband to his farm. That dress is just *too* elegant, Kitty, but I think it might not be suitable for milking cows in!"

"It is no matter, I shall burn it as soon as I may," Catherine replied.

Susannah gasped, and the duchess bridled angrily.

"You ungrateful girl!" she exclaimed. "I am appalled. As for you, Susannah, I will have you remember that Mr. Woodmere is a *gentleman* farmer. Catherine will not have to demean herself by performing any such menial tasks, and it would reflect very poorly on all of us if anyone heard you speak so. Now let us go down. I believe the carriages are ready."

Catherine followed her stepmother and stepsister out of the room, reflecting that the two were the least of her troubles. Just a few minutes, and she would be alone with Philip, and she still didn't know quite what she would say to him, or how.

Somehow she managed to descend the stairs without falling, despite her shaky limbs, and to put the smile firmly back onto her face before the party assembled in the hall could see her agitation. She and Philip accepted more wishes for a good journey and a happy marriage, and finally went down the front steps toward the awaiting carriages.

Two coaches stood before the castle, both with the ducal crest on them, His Grace having decided this would make the greater impression on the assembled party. Catherine knew that she and Philip were to ride in the first. A maid from the castle who was to wait on her during the journey rode in the second, with their baggage.

The final moment came. Catherine exchanged perfunctory embraces with the assembled Harcourts, then real ones with Philip's family, almost breaking down

when Lizzie flung her arms around her neck and reminded her to take good care of Philip.

As they drove off, she forced herself to smile and
wave at the assembled well-wishers. As soon as they
were out of sight, she slumped back into a corner of
the carriage. Finally, she was alone with Philip, but
she did not dare to even look at him, for fear she might
start weeping with all the accumulated tension of the
past week.

They drove on in an awkward silence, until Catherine could bear it no longer. She turned toward Philip,
and saw him watching her from the opposite corner of
the carriage. He looked tense and weary, as if he
hadn't slept for a week, and no more at ease than she
was. Could she succeed in bridging this frightening
distance between them?

"Philip," she began, and had to lick her lips, which
had gone dry with nervousness. "It is time I told you
the truth about everything, about—about what happened with Verwood."

"No!"

She started at the vehemence in his voice.

"No," he repeated more softly, but his voice was
hoarse with revulsion. "Not now. Not here."

"I am so sorry," she said, mortified. "After all you
have endured today, I suppose you would rather be left
alone. I can see how unhappy you are. We must talk
later, but do know this, that if you wish for your freedom, I shall not stand in your way."

"What?" he asked, straightening up.

"If you want an—an annulment, or a divorce, I am
prepared to do whatever is necessary to help."

He stared at her for a stunned instant, brows drawing together.

"Annulment! Divorce!" he exploded. "Don't even speak of such things!"

She shrank from the unleashed fury in his voice. She hadn't known he was capable of such anger. Half consciously, she crossed her arms in front of herself in a protective gesture.

"I know it will cause a scandal," she said. "All I wished to say was that if you wished to be free of me . . ."

Her voice broke.

"I've no such wish," he replied, and turned away from her. She heard him breathe deeply, as if in an effort to master his temper. A moment later, the carriage slowed, and Philip ordered the coachman to stop.

Catherine watched him anxiously as he turned back to her.

"I should not have shouted at you," he said in a carefully controlled voice. "We are in Little Hayfield now. I am going to hire a horse and ride from here. Do you wish for the maid to come forward and ride with you?"

She shook her head. Wordlessly, she watched him get out of the carriage. Soon, they were on their way again. She caught a brief glimpse of Philip riding ahead, and sank back into her seat, heavy-hearted. She had made a botch of things once more. He could not even bear to share a carriage with her.

For the next few hours, she clung to one remaining hope. Philip had not said he would never listen to her story. It seemed he was eager to return home, for they pressed on at a good pace. When they finally stopped, she thought his ride had done him some good.

"I did not mean to frighten you earlier, Catherine," he said as he came forward to escort her into the inn where they were to dine. "You know I would never hurt you."

"Of course not," she said.

"You were overwrought. It has been a difficult week, and we are both weary. If we try to speak now, one of us might say something we would later regret. Can you wait until tomorrow, when we return to the Hall?"

She nodded, though his gentle, sensible words nearly overset her. She would rather he had upbraided her than treat her with this distant kindness, and felt an insane urge to throw herself on his chest in a wild attempt to regain their former closeness. She held back, fearing he would despise such weak behavior.

After a brief dinner, they resumed their journey, Philip having informed her that he hoped to cover several more stages before stopping for the night. It should have been no surprise, and yet Catherine felt both hurt and mortified when Philip engaged them two rooms at the inn near Preston where they stopped at dusk. After he bade her a polite good night, and the maid from Whitgrave helped her prepare for bed, Catherine climbed into the comfortable four-poster. She lay awake for a long time, hoping against hope that Philip would change his mind, and come to join her. Finally, she realized he would not.

Although she was tired from the strain of the day, still she could not sleep. She tossed about for what seemed like ages, drifting into dreams of Philip's arms around her, and rousing again to the bitter knowledge that she was alone on her wedding night. Finally, she dozed off sometime in the early morning, and awakened only when the sun was already riding high in the heavens.

Mercifully, Philip had not sent anyone to rouse her, and did not complain about their late start. Again, he rode, allowing Catherine more time than she wished to think about everything that had happened.

She was as determined as ever to explain everything to Philip. How he would react to the knowledge of her illegitimacy, and to her lack of faith, she did not know. All she did know was that she could not bear the thought of living with him as if they were strangers. If he had lost all affection for her, as seemed likely, she would have to reopen the subject of divorce. Aside from his aversion to the scandal, Philip would probably be glad to have her gone.

Miserably, she contemplated her future. With a sharp pang, she realized that Juliana and Penelope would not be permitted to associate with her. As a scandalous divorced woman, she would have to live beyond the pale of respectable society. The best she could hope for was to go live on the Continent somewhere. The duke's pride had forced him to provide her with a substantial dowry; she was certain Philip would let her have it. She could buy a small house, with a garden and a pianoforte, and hope that in time she would find some new friends, and that her own heart would heal. How bleak it all seemed!

The sun was just setting over the western fells when she reached Woodmere Hall. Surrounded by its ancient oaks, aglow with the setting sun, the old stone house had never looked more homelike.

Philip, who had ridden ahead to prepare the household, now appeared in the doorway. His hair was damp; apparently he had bathed after his long ride. As he came forward to hand her down from the carriage, she noticed he looked more cheerful than before.

"Welcome home, love," he said, and she nearly broke down at the warm clasp of his hand and the unexpected endearment. Was it a mere slip of the tongue?

She went with him into the house. Despite the late hour, all the servants had gathered in the hall to welcome her as their new mistress. She was already acquainted with most of them, so it was a mere formality, yet she felt warmed by their reception. She was also surprised to see Jemima among the assembled household staff.

"Good evening, me lady," said Jemima when Catherine came to her. "The master thought you might like to have me as your maid."

"I am very glad to see you, Jemima," she replied.

Meanwhile, Philip had given orders for her trunks to be brought up to the master bedchamber. Now Catherine realized that at the Hall, unlike grander homes, there were no separate bedchambers for master and mistress. Did Philip intend to follow that custom, or did he plan some other arrangement?

He turned to her and gave a slight smile.

"Do you wish for anything, Catherine? Something to eat or drink before we retire?"

She shook her head, too unstrung to even speak. He spoke as if he planned to join her. Had she misunderstood?

"Well, then, Jemima will show you up to our room."

She turned and followed Jemima up the staircase and into a large corner bedchamber. As it was a cool evening, a small, cheery fire had been kindled in the massive stone fireplace, which looked as if it could give ample heat even for the coldest of nights. Catherine caught the fragrance of roses, mingled with the spicier clove scent of pinks, and saw that several bowls of the flowers decorated the room. Had Philip ordered them? Or were they just a welcoming gesture from the housekeeper, or Jemima, perhaps? Across the room, she noticed a cushioned seat built under the window, and another door sharing a wall with the fireplace.

"That leads to the master's dressing room," said Jemima in answer to her questioning look.

From what Jemima said, it sounded as if Philip had had his things brought over from the room he had occupied at the other end of the house. Catherine tried to curb her rising hopes, telling herself it only meant he wished to keep up the pretense that theirs was an ordinary marriage. No doubt he would actually sleep elsewhere. In all likelihood that door would never be used.

She watched as Jemima gestured toward a dressing table and wardrobe on the other side of the room, informing her that this was to be her dressing area. Jemima came forward to unbutton Catherine's traveling dress, and took the opportunity to wish her happy on her wedding. Catherine forced herself to smile and accepted Jemima's good wishes, and listen as Jemima chattered on about her own plans.

"Do you know, me lady, Ned and I are going to be wed as well!"

"I am very happy for you both," she replied, stepping out of her dress.

"It's all the master's doing. He's hired Ned to help tend the orchards and the garden here, though he'll still go back and do for the ladies at the cottage too," said Jemima, as she brought out a white nightgown with long sleeves and a frill at the neck. "Who would 'ave thought it—two Londoners like us, settling down in a place like this. But I don't mind telling you we are happy as grigs!"

Catherine smiled at Jemima as she helped her out of her underclothes, and into the nightgown. It was a small relief to know that at least some good had come of all this.

She sat down at the dressing table. As Jemima brushed and braided her hair, she took the opportunity to study the room a little more closely. The walls were covered in an ivy-patterned paper; the curtains and bed hangings were of a rich wine color, edged with dark forest green. Several watercolor sketches of fruit and birds, in pairs of male and female, decorated the walls.

After Jemima had finished with her hair, Catherine washed her face and hands, then got up from the dressing table.

"Will you be going straight to bed, me lady, or do you wish for a dressing gown?"

Catherine looked over at the enormous four-poster that dominated the room. Like the rest of the furnishings, it was made of oak. It was dark with age and heavily carved with flowers, fruit, and pairs of birds. More symbols of love and fertility. Generations of Woodmeres must have lain together and loved each other in this bed. Catherine felt like an interloper to even think of sleeping in it alone.

"I would like to sit up for a while," she said.

She pulled on the blue satin dressing gown Jemima held out to her. After bidding her maid good night, she went to the window seat and sat down. Looking out, she saw the outline of the hills behind the house, and beyond them, a starry sky so beautiful it made her want to weep.

She turned away from the view. She could hear

voices from the adjacent dressing room: Philip's low accents, answered by another male voice, his manservant, perhaps. So he *was* using the dressing room. Again, hope flickered, then she reminded herself what had happened last night. Could she really hope he would come here to sleep?

Soon the voices stilled. Catherine waited for a few more minutes, and concluded drearily that Philip must have gone to bed. She should have been weary from traveling, but instead she felt horridly restless. Finally, she told herself it was time to stop hoping Philip would come to her. It was too late; she would have to wait until tomorrow to talk to him. It was time to stop staring at that connecting door, for it was not going to open.

Then she heard a knock.

Sixteen

Catherine's heart pounded furiously as she stared at the door.

There was another knock. This time, she managed to utter some faint words of welcome.

The door opened, and Philip entered. He wore a burgundy dressing gown, and under it a white nightshirt that contrasted starkly against his tanned skin. He gazed at her intently, his eyes full of some mysterious emotion she hardly dared guess at.

Her Corsair, dark and masculine. And he was in her room. *Their* room.

Her mouth went suddenly dry. Then she reminded herself that he might not be here to stay. More likely he only wished to talk.

For a moment, they stared at each other, and the only sound was the soft crackle of the fire. Then Philip broke the silence.

"Please don't be frightened of me, Catherine," he said softly.

She shook her head, but could not say anything. She longed to run across the room, throw herself on his chest, beg his forgiveness, beg him to kiss her and . . . No, she could not do it. She would explain herself calmly and rationally; she would not embarrass him by making such a fool of herself.

"I'll not force myself upon you," Philip said, advancing across the room toward her. "But I do ask this, that we at least share a bed."

She stared at him, aghast, her resolution faltering. He didn't wish to make love to her, but he wanted them to share a bed anyway? Was it to prevent the servants and his family from suspecting that theirs was not a real marriage? It was insane. She could not do it. She could not lie with him and keep from putting her arms around him and begging him to love her again.

"I cannot," she cried. "You do not need to do this, Philip. You can divorce me. I know it will cause a great deal of talk, but—"

"I told you I don't wish for a divorce," he said, sitting down on the edge of the bed, across from the window seat. He did not sound as angry as he had yesterday, but sad and weary. "I am sorry I shouted at you yesterday. You wanted to tell me something. Would you like to do so now?"

She nodded. She had waited a week to do this, and yet now she found it difficult to begin.

He waited patiently for a moment, then spoke. "Back at the Fox and Grouse, you told me you'd gone willingly with Verwood, and that you would explain it to me. If it would help you to speak of what happened, I will listen."

The tightness in his voice and the tension in his body revealed the effort it cost him to make the offer.

"The day Verwood came here, he asked me to run away with him," she began, her voice shaking a little. "I refused to go, but then he told me something— something about my mother."

She swallowed nervously, and steeled herself to

continue. "He told me she betrayed the duke. I am not his daughter. My father is a musician His Grace hired to entertain guests at the Castle, some twenty years ago."

"Verwood told you this? And you believed him?"

"Yes. It explains so much: my music, the fact that I bear no resemblance to the duke. The way he has always favored Susannah and Cedric over me . . ."

"This is why you ran off with Verwood? Because you thought I'd care about your birth?" Philip got up and began to pace the length of the room between the bed and the window seat. "Well, I don't give a damn! Now that I know the duke, and have seen how he treats you, I'm glad you've none of his blood in your veins!"

He came back to stand near her, looking down at her with a deep reproach in his eyes. "You should have known I wouldn't care."

"But it was not just my birth." she replied. "It was what my mother did."

"I don't find it so shocking," he said, sitting back down opposite her. "While I was in Derbyshire I learned a few things about your father. From what I've heard, he has never had the slightest notion of fidelity. I don't doubt your mother married him, thinking that she loved him, and was deeply hurt when she learned of his mistresses. I suspect she fell in love with that musician of hers, and would have gone off with him, had she not thought staying would be better for *you.* She must have been desperately unhappy; we cannot judge her. Nor should you think you will be the same."

Catherine's heart nearly stopped beating. Perhaps Philip *would* understand what had happened.

"That was what I feared," she admitted. "The duke and duchess always called me wanton and abandoned.

Last Season, when Staverton kissed me, I felt . . . feelings that seemed wanton and abandoned, at least I thought so at the time. Then when Verwood tried to—to seduce me, I found I could not let him. I only wanted you."

"That is when you ran away from him?"

She nodded.

"Dear God! You are no wanton, Catherine. Damn those who have made you think so!" He buried his face in his hands for a moment. "When I think of all that's happened . . ."

Lifting his head again, he said, "I wish you had trusted me. I wish you had believed in our love."

"I know I should have," she said, aching for the pain she heard in his voice. "I think I must be doomed to cause grief to everyone in my life, even those I love best."

Philip gazed at her for a moment, then arose from the bed and came to sit beside her on the window seat. "Don't say that," he said. "You have made me happy from the first day we met, when you saved Lizzie's life. Do you think that means nothing? Besides all the things you've done for Marianne, and the boys."

She looked down. Did she dare hope? He could be saying all these things merely to console her, out of kindness, or pity.

"I have hurt you so much," she said. "Do you think you can forgive me?"

She began to shake, and the tears she had been unable to shed over the past week threatened to gush forth.

"I forgive you, Catherine," he said, putting a tentative arm around her. "Can you forgive me? I failed you, too. I should have believed you when you told me about your family. I thought you were exaggerating. I didn't know how unloving, how cold your life had been. I will make it better. I swear it!"

"You still love me? After all I have done?" she asked, her voice breaking.

"It doesn't matter. *Nothing* that has happened matters. I am here now, and I love you."

Relief flooded through her; with it, her fragile defenses crumbled. Sobs wracked her body, but Philip held her, and she cried into his shoulder in a blessed catharsis.

"Cathy, Cathy," he murmured. "It will be well, I promise. I love you, Cathy," he repeated over and over, rocking her in his arms.

Finally, the storm passed through her, leaving only joy in its wake. She brushed her face against his dressing gown, taking comfort in its softness against her cheek, then lifted her head to look into his face. There she saw the ravages of the torment he had suffered, but also a dawning joy that matched her own.

She tilted her head up and kissed him softly, hoping to banish the final vestiges of sadness from his face. At first, he sat perfectly still, as if surprised by her action. Then he began to gently kiss her in return. Desire stirred inside her, and she wondered at his unusual restraint.

Yearning for more, she parted her lips, inviting him to deepen their kiss. He gave a shudder, deep in his body, then his tongue sought hers. She closed her eyes and kissed him back fiercely, hungrily, with all the pent-up longing of the past week.

After a moment, he slackened his hold. Catherine felt his hands move up to her shoulders, and opened her eyes. He was gazing at her, eyes dark with passion.

A warm, pleasurable blush arose in her cheeks as he pushed the dressing gown down off her shoulders, down to her elbows. She pulled her arms out of the sleeves, letting the gown pool around her waist. Philip untied his own dressing gown and shrugged out of it. She couldn't help staring. The top of his nightshirt was unbuttoned, revealing a portion of tanned neck and chest, the fire throwing golden highlights over the flat surfaces and deeply shading the musculature beneath.

Philip gathered her into his arms again, and they embraced, with only the two thin layers of fabric between them. Holding one arm firmly around her, he stroked her hair with the other hand, running it down to the end of her braid. For a moment, he fumbled behind her as he unfastened the braid, then combed his fingers through her hair until it hung loosely down her back. He pulled away for a moment to gaze at her.

"Oh, I've longed to see you like this, love," he said, voice husky with desire.

She gazed back into his beloved face again, then back down at the tantalizing opening of his nightshirt. Through the fine linen, she could just follow the whisper of dark, curling hair leading down the center of his chest. She realized the thin cotton of her nightgown was just as revealing of her charms, and rejoiced in Philip's obvious enjoyment of the sight. This was not wrong, this pleasure they shared in each other. It was *meant*.

He put an arm around her again, slipped his other hand under her knees, and carried her across the room toward the bed. He placed her down upon it, got in beside her, and pulled the covers over them. She rolled, turning to face him. He looked at her longingly for a moment, then put his arms around her again,

drawing her in close so that she felt his warmth along
the entire length of her body. He began to run his
hands up and down her, exploring every curve through
the thin barrier of her nightgown. A shudder of delight
spread through her, then to her dismay, he pulled away.

"It is too much, love? Should I stop?" he asked.

She stared at him. In the firelight, he looked absurdly concerned. She didn't know whether to laugh or
scream.

"No. Please do not stop," she said, trying to pull
him back toward her.

He sighed as if in relief, and gathered her close
again. This time, she shyly began to explore his contours even as he was exploring hers. She had barely
touched him when he drew in a sudden breath and
gently pushed her onto her back.

She wondered what he would do next. He raised
himself up on one elbow and carefully unbuttoned the
top button of her nightgown. Excitement quickened
her breath, but she smiled up at him, silently encouraging him as his large but deft fingers undid one button after another. Finally, he reached the last one, just
above her waist, then he hesitantly trailed a finger
down the long, narrow ribbon of flesh revealed between the folds of thin white fabric.

He withdrew his hand, to Catherine's disappointment. Then he sat up to remove his own nightshirt.
Helplessly, she admired his broad, muscular body for
a brief moment before he dropped back onto his elbow
again and pulled the covers back over them.

"I love you, Catherine," he murmured, and kissed
the base of her throat. Then he pulled the sides of her
nightgown apart.

She gave a little moan of delight as his lips and

hands roved over her, kissing and caressing every bit of her exposed, sensitive skin. She sat up to help him as he tugged the nightgown down to her waist, then blushingly, eagerly burrowed into his arms, savoring the wondrous joy of his uncovered body against hers.

A new, thrumming excitement stole over her as she felt his hand tugging at the skirt of her nightgown. He pulled the folds of cotton toward her waist, stroking up her thigh until he reached a place that positively ached for his caress. She had never imagined he could touch her this way, making her tremble and moan with the delight of it.

Then through her delirium, she remembered that there was something she needed to tell him, that he still did not know how her night with Verwood had ended.

"Philip," she said, drawing back slightly.

"What is wrong?" He stilled his hand, and she almost cried out for him to move it again. No, she needed to tell him.

"Verwood and I . . ." she began, struggling for the right words, distracted by the weight of Philip's hand lying on her. "We—"

"Don't speak of him!" he said gruffly. "Think only of me, that I love you."

He resumed his caresses, fondling her with tender thoroughness, leaving no sensitive spot untouched. Instinctively, she reached an arm under him. Clinging to the support of his firm, warm torso, she gripped him ever more tightly as her pleasure reached new peaks. Finally she twisted and cried out as a sudden sweet rapture overwhelmed all her senses.

She sank back onto the bed, pulses still racing. For a moment, Philip lay beside her, holding her as she recovered her breath. Then he shifted and moved over her. Replete with pleasure, serenely happy, she readied herself for what was to come. Still, when it did, she could not help stiffening, nor letting out a small cry.

Philip withdrew from her instantly.

"Cathy! I thought—I was sure—" he stammered, then paused to take a deep breath. "Have I hurt you?"

She shook her head, smiling up at him to reassure him.

"Why did you not tell me?"

"I tried, but you stopped me."

"So Verwood did not force himself on you?" he asked, an eager gladness in his voice.

"No," she said. "I only ran away from him to get back to you. He tried to stop me, but only for my safety. Verwood might seduce, but he would never force a woman. He slept on the floor that night."

"Thank God!" he said, lying down beside her again. He put an arm around her and gathered her toward him. She laid her head on his chest, and felt him let out another deep, ragged breath.

"You don't know what I suffered, when I thought of you, frightened, hurt, in his control," he said. "You looked so miserable that morning I was certain he'd ravished you. It was the greatest agony I've ever felt, to know that I was too late to prevent it. I feared you thought yourself ruined, and wanted no man to touch you again. I thought that was why you resisted marrying me."

"Was that why you did not come to me last night?" she asked.

"Yes. My only thought was to get you home as quickly as I could, and hope that with time, patience and love would overcome whatever Verwood had done."

A tear rolled down her cheek. As it splashed down onto his chest, Philip turned his head toward hers.

"Why do you cry, love?"

"No one has ever loved me so."

She wiped away a second tear, then put her arms about him, embracing him with all her strength. His arms came around her, and he shifted her so that she lay on top of him. A slight draft blew through the room, and Catherine caught the scent of their passion, mingling with the fragrance of the roses and clove-pinks. She lowered her head to give Philip a long, deep kiss, and felt his chest rise and fall more quickly beneath her.

"Shall we try again?" she asked, boldly smiling down at him.

Instantly, he rolled them both over so that she was on her back once more. He hovered over her for an instant, love and desire shining from his eyes. Then he entered her, more gently this time. Now there was no pain, only a wonderful sense of closeness.

He began to move slowly within her, and she was unsure what she should do. Following her impulses, she tried to match his rhythm, and felt a new, deeper pleasure building within her. Philip's breathing quickened. His face contorted in an expression of sweet torment, and she reveled in the awareness that she was giving him pleasure as well. A moment later, he cried her name, and collapsed onto her. He took a few ragged breaths, then lifted himself back onto his arms and settled himself by her side.

"I love you, Cathy," he murmured.

He laid his head against her breast, and she ran a

hand through his tousled hair, feeling a serenity she had never known before.

"I love you, too," she replied, continuing to stroke his hair in a silence broken only by the sound of the fire.

Gradually, Philip's breathing deepened. Catherine knew he was close to sleep, but she did not mind. A blessed tiredness was stealing over her as well. She had never imagined what a joy it would be to curl up beside one's husband to sleep after passion was sated.

Drowsily, she wondered if they might have just started a child. It would be glorious if they had, but it did not really matter. They would have many days and nights for joy and passion. Finally, she knew that she and Philip would share a lifetime of happy tomorrows.

ABOUT THE AUTHOR

Elena Greene lives with her husband and two daughters in upstate New York. She is the author of two Regency romances, LORD LANGDON'S KISS and THE INCORRIGIBLE LADY CATHERINE. She loves to hear from readers and you may write to her at P.O. Box 535, Apalachin, NY 13732. Please include a self-addressed envelope if you wish for a reply. You can also send Elena e-mail at *egreene@stny.rr.com* and visit her home page at *http://home.stny.rr.com/elenagreene*.

More Zebra Regency Romances

Embrace the Romances of
Shannon Drake

Merlin's Legacy

A Series From
Quinn Taylor Evans